Scott

BASKET FEVER

BASKET FEVER

by Robert Sidney Bowen

illustrated by
James Dunnington

A WHITMAN BOOK

Western Publishing Company, Inc.
Racine, Wisconsin

WHITMAN is a registered trademark
of Western Publishing Company, Inc.

CONTENTS

BASKET FEVER

1 A Premonition

JEFF BATES drank the last of his orange juice, set the glass down on the breakfast table, and stared moodily out the window. Outside, a bright December morning sun was striving to reduce the biting chill built up during the hours of darkness. The first snow of winter had yet to come to Bedford City, but the way the mercury plummeted after sundown was a pretty good indication that the white stuff was not too far away.

Jeff, a reasonably good-looking youth approaching

his seventeenth birthday, had thick chestnut hair, dark brown eyes, a rugged chin, and a mouth that was quick to smile. He was six feet two inches tall, well boned, and muscular. His arms, however, were longer than those of the average youth his height, and his hands were much bigger. In short, he possessed the ideal build for a basketball player, and he loved the game. But as yet he had failed to make the Bedford High School team. Last year, as a sophomore, he had not survived the final squad cut, and now, as a junior, he was more than a little worried about his chances.

Seated across the table from him was his aunt, Kate Martin, an attractive woman in her early thirties, the sister of his dead mother. Eight years ago, when an airliner crash had taken the lives of his father and mother, Aunt Kate had come to keep house and be a family to him during his growing-up years. At first it had been a strain for them both, but as time passed, a bond of respect and affection almost as strong and enduring as that between real mother and son formed between them.

For a few moments Kate Martin studied her nephew in speculative silence.

"What's the problem?" she suddenly asked.

Jeff turned his head to give her a wry smile.

"Nothing much," he said. "I'm just scared stiff, that's all."

"Scared?" his aunt echoed. "Of what?"

"That I won't make it today," Jeff told her.

14

"Make what today?" Kate Martin probed.

Jeff snapped open his mouth but closed it just as quickly.

"The final squad cut," he said, as patiently as he could. "I told you last night, don't you remember? Today is ax day. Coach Parks is posting the names of the fourteen lucky guys on the gym bulletin board just before practice this afternoon."

Kate Martin formed a silent O with her lips and nodded.

"Now I understand," she said. Then she added with a frown, "But why are you scared? Last night, as I recall, you were pretty confident you'd make the cut. Why the switch this morning?"

Jeff hunched a shoulder. "That was last night," he grunted absently. He licked his lips and gave a little twist of his head. "Do you believe in dreams, Aunt Kate?" he suddenly asked.

"Do I *what?*"

"Believe in dreams."

Kate Martin nodded. "That's what I thought you said. Well, I'd say that depends. If they're good ones I might tend to lean that way. But why such a question?"

"My dreams last night weren't good," Jeff said with an emphatic shake of his head. "They were terrible! I woke up in a cold sweat. Couldn't get them out of my mind and go back to sleep, they were so darn real. Know what I mean?"

"Not yet," Kate Martin said, watching him. "Perhaps

15

when you tell me about it. . . ."

Jeff paused a moment to marshal his thoughts.

"I guess I must sound nuts," he suddenly blurted. "Everybody has nightmares, of course, but this one was different—ten times worse than any I've ever had—so real it still scares me now. It was—well, like I was living in the future and seeing all that was happening. You know?"

"No," his aunt said bluntly. "But go on. What was it all about?"

"It was this afternoon," Jeff said. "The final cut, I mean. Well, I dreamed that I went into the gym to take a look at the list of the fourteen guys who'd survived the cut. Everybody else was there, including Coach Parks, standing around talking. But when I came in everybody shut up and sort of moved to one side so that I could walk right up to the bulletin board. Well, I did, and when I got close enough to take a look, there was my name on the list. It was the last name, but it was there. Boy, did I feel good!"

He paused to take a quick breath and unconsciously pressed his clenched fist into the palm of the other hand.

"Then it happened," he continued. "Frank Ames suddenly appeared beside me, pulled a foot-long pencil out of his pocket, reached out, and scratched my name off the list! Well, that made me see red, and I made a grab for Ames. But before I could, Coach Parks grabbed me and yanked me away and shouted that he'd *told* Ames to scratch my name off the list. I asked him why, and he said he'd made a mistake. He'd put fifteen names on the list, when there should have been only fourteen. And since mine was the fifteenth name, it had to come off. And that was that."

Jeff paused again for breath and drew a slightly trembling hand down the side of his face. His aunt frowned but didn't speak.

"Well, I took another look and counted the names," he went on. "And, sure enough, mine was the fifteenth name. I turned to protest to Parks, but he put me off, saying that it was final. I'd been cut from the squad. Then, with a crazy laugh, he told me I shouldn't feel too bad, since I hadn't made the cut last year, either. So what was I squawking about? Well, that really steamed me up. I was starting to yell—to give it to him hot and heavy—when I woke up in a cold sweat."

Jeff stopped talking and slowly rubbed his palms together as he looked expectantly at his aunt.

"Well?" he prompted when she remained silent.

His aunt raised her brows innocently. "Well what?"

He gaped and sputtered the words out. "The dream, of course! Don't you see how real it was—why it bugs me so? It's like a—a premonition!"

Kate Martin eyed him gravely for a moment, then snorted. "Rubbish!" she said tartly. "It was only a silly dream!"

Jeff blinked. Then he sighed heavily and slumped in his chair.

"Thanks a bunch!" he moaned. "That really cheers

17

me up tremendously, you know!"

"Oh, come off it, Jeff," his aunt scoffed. "Stop feeling sorry for yourself. You're making a big thing out of nothing! You had a bad dream. So what? Forget it!"

"If only I could!" Jeff groaned. He shook his head and tapped it with a finger. "It's like it's stuck up here. I can't seem to get rid of it. It's so *real*—every part of it. I—"

"Every part?" Kate Martin checked him. "Does Frank Ames carry around a foot-long pencil? And—" She checked herself and slapped the table. "That's it!" Kate declared. "The subconscious at work!"

"Sub who?" Jeff grunted, peering at her.

"This Frank Ames," his aunt said. "You've mentioned him before. Isn't he the one boy in your class you don't like? The one with the ugly temper or something?"

"I never said Frank Ames had an ugly temper," Jeff told her. "Maybe he has one; he's a hard guy to figure. He's a real loner and keeps it that way. You just can't get close to him. I've tried, and so have some of the other guys, but it's no go. He cuts you stone dead and walks away. Thing is, though, I don't like the guy, but I don't dislike him, either. He goes his way and I go mine, and that's all there is to it."

His aunt gave a short laugh and gestured with her hands. "I guess that takes care of that," she said.

"Come again? What do you mean?"

"A very weighty idea I had," Kate Martin said with

a faint grimace. "I thought that possibly this Frank Ames. . . ." She stopped with a shake of her head. "No, it's too silly," she said.

"No, tell me what you were going to say," Jeff put in quickly. "What about Ames?"

"Well, if you really want to know," his aunt said with a shrug, "I was about to say that sometimes when something is bothering us subconsciously, it becomes magnified all out of proportion when it comes to us in a dream. I simply thought that, because of your dislike for Frank Ames and perhaps because you're worried that he'll beat you out for a place on the team, he'd naturally become the villain in your dream. Do you see what I mean?"

"Kind of, I guess," Jeff said slowly. "Only it isn't like that. Like I said, I couldn't care less about the guy one way or the other. And as for worrying about him beating *me* out for the team, that's plain crazy."

"Why is it?" Kate Martin wanted to know.

"No contest, that's why," he told her. "Ames is the best basketball player in the school. He was on the team last year, and he was runner-up for the most valuable player award. *Me* beat out Frank Ames? Forget it!"

"Good idea," his aunt said with a nod. "In fact, let's forget this whole silly conversation. Neither of us has made very much sense, I'm afraid. So let's cross it all out. Agreed?"

He frowned and started to speak. At that moment the toot of a car horn sounded from the driveway.

19

"That's Paul," he said, pushing back his chair. "See you later."

His aunt rose, too, and walked with him into the living room, where he collected his school books from a table.

"Call me at the office, will you?" she asked as he moved toward the front door. "When you find out, I mean. I'd like to know as soon as I can."

"Will do," Jeff said and pulled open the door.

"And, Jeff?"

He paused and half turned. "Yes, Aunt Kate?"

"Lots of luck," she said softly.

He grinned in answer, but it required effort. For some reason, he suddenly felt a bit queasy in the pit of his stomach.

"Thanks," he managed to say as he turned and went out the door.

2   *End Name on the List*

CLOSING THE FRONT DOOR behind him, Jeff went down the porch steps and across the lawn to a slightly battered-looking Chevrolet in the driveway. Seated behind the wheel was Paul Young, his closest friend since grammar school days. He was about Jeff's height, fair haired, and built lean and wiry. He, too, was a hopeful candidate for the Bedford High basketball team. When Jeff got into the car he gave Paul an inquiring, searching look.

"How'd *you* sleep last night?" he asked, trying to sound casual.

"Like a baby," was Paul's quick reply. "How else?"

Jeff snorted. "Now I'll tell one!" he said. They started backing out of the driveway. Jeff grinned at him. "Really—you, too, huh?"

"Right," Paul admitted. "Tossed and turned all night long. Couldn't get the cut off my mind. That's what bugs me. Letting it get to me. Plain stupid!"

"How so?" Jeff asked.

"Because it's stupid! So I don't make the cut. So what? It's the end of the world? Nuts!"

"It could be for me," Jeff murmured, as though to himself. "Boy, if I don't make it this year, I don't know what I'll do. Cut my throat, maybe."

Paul Young glanced at him and chuckled. "You and Frank Ames!"

Jeff jerked his head around, his face tight. "What's that supposed to mean?"

Paul took his eyes off the road just long enough for a startled look at Jeff. "Hey, what's with you?" he exclaimed.

"No jokes," Jeff said. "Just a question. What's Ames got to do with me?"

"Who said he had anything—"

"You did!" Jeff shot back. "Just now. You said, 'You and Frank Ames.' Why?"

The other youth opened his mouth to speak but checked it. Instead he waited until he'd passed a car just ahead and swung back into the lane again.

"You're really shook up this morning, aren't you?" he grunted. "Relax, pal! I only said that because you two guys are the ones so hooked on basketball. It's like a religion or something for you two. Nothing else matters."

"That's bad?" Jeff challenged.

"No, it's wonderful!" Paul snapped. Mounting annoyance showed in his face. "The best thing ever! Okay? Satisfied?"

Jeff thought of telling Paul about his crazy nightmare but rejected the idea. He reached over and gave his best friend a playful rap on the arm.

"Sure, and I'm sorry," he said. "I shouldn't have popped off like that. I'm kind of edgy this morning, and you linking Ames and me together rubbed me the wrong way, I guess. Know what I mean?"

"Yeah, sure," Paul said. "Forget it. I don't like Frank any more than you do. Just meant you two were the craziest about basketball, that's all."

"Funny thing," Jeff said, as though he hadn't been listening. "I was telling my aunt at breakfast that I didn't like or dislike that guy. And it's true. He's one heck of a basketball player, but as a guy he's a nothing—to me, anyway."

"To a lot of people," Paul added. "Like about everybody at school. You know, if Ames was somebody else, he could be the most popular guy at Bedford."

"But he isn't," Jeff pointed out. "He's Frank Ames,

23

the total loner, the mystery guy that nobody can figure. I wonder why. What do you suppose makes a guy like that tick?"

For a moment or two Paul didn't say anything. He concentrated on his driving but presently shrugged. "Search me," he said. "Maybe he's ashamed of something and tries to cover it up by going around acting tough, with a chip on his shoulder."

"No, that's wrong," Jeff said. "He really doesn't act tough—not like he's itching for a fight, I mean. You just think it from those eyes of his. They can sure look mean and ugly. But it stops there. He doesn't say anything. Just gives you those eyes and walks away. You just can't figure what's going on with him, period."

"But there's something that makes him that way," Paul insisted. "And I still think it's because he's ashamed of something."

"Like what?"

"Like his background, for one thing," Paul said after a moment's thought. "Add it up. Comes from the South Side, and you know what it's like down there. Crummy tenement houses, some with no heat, eight and ten people living in the same room, and all that. Must be really tough on a kid, living down there and having to fight for everything just to be able to survive."

Jeff laughed. "Boy, you sound like you're running for mayor or something." Then he said soberly, "But I suppose you're right. It must be lousy for a kid to grow up in a place like that, especially when he goes to school and sees the clothes and all the stuff the other kids have. Yeah, maybe it's like you say. He's ashamed. But, there are other guys at Bedford that come from that area, too, and none that I know are like Ames. So it may be something more than just being ashamed of where he comes from."

"No argument from me," Paul said with a shrug. "Probably is. Maybe pride. I mean, maybe he's the kind of guy who resents help, no matter what. Wants to make it all on his own. And maybe, never having had anything, he gets suspicious of anyone who tries to give him something for nothing—even ordinary friendship."

"You can say that again!" Jeff breathed. "The suspicious part, I mean. That's the look he gives you every time you open your mouth, even only to say hi. Suspicious that you're up to something. That's it, all right. Always afraid you might be trying to pull something on him. And he's crazy to think like that. That's what beats me. What's he got that anybody wants, anyway?"

"Nothing, but maybe he doesn't look at it that way," Paul said. "Maybe he doesn't care a hoot what anybody says or does. He could have his own thing going for him, and that's all that counts right now."

"What has he got going for him?" Jeff asked. "You mean something to do with his basketball playing?"

Paul Young hunched a shoulder. "I wasn't thinking of anything special," he answered. "But, now that you mention it, it could be basketball. Yeah! I kind of think it is. Must be!"

Jeff turned in the seat to give Paul a shrewd look. "I get the idea you know something I don't," he said. "What?"

"I don't *know* a thing," Paul replied after a few moments of silence. "It's just that I suddenly remembered something a guy told me about Ames. Nick Reno. He graduated last year. You remember him?"

Jeff shook his head. "A blank. What about him?"

"He sat beside me in second-year French," Paul said. "He was from the South Side, too. Lived on the same street as Frank, I think he said. Anyway, he knew Frank pretty well, and it was the day after the Newton game last year—the one when Frank racked up thirty-one points and just about won the game all by himself."

"Yeah, I remember that game," Jeff said as the other youth paused for breath. "So?"

"Well, we were talking about the game," Paul continued, "and Nick said that Frank's one and only ambition was to make himself such a hotshot in high-school basketball that he'd be sure to get a flock of scholarship offers from colleges. He'd set his sights on getting into college that way, and nothing, but nothing, was going to stop him. It was the only way a fellow in his position could make college. Money and top school grades were out, as far as he was concerned. So he was going to make basketball do it for him."

"You can't blame the guy for that," Jeff said impulsively. "More power to him!"

Paul gave him a surprised look, but he didn't say

anything, because at that moment they reached the entrance to the Bedford High School parking lot, and traffic was heavy. Instead he kept his thoughts to himself and concentrated on driving his car follow-the-leader style into the parking area and finding a vacant slot.

"So how about it?" he said when they were parked. "Do we meet in front of the gym after last class, or have you got something else planned?"

"No, I'm clean," Jeff said. "We'll meet. And, Paul—"

"Yeah?"

Jeff held up crossed fingers. "Here's luck—for both of us."

Paul grinned and seemed to gulp a little. "Right. *Both* of us!" he said a bit hoarsely.

They got out of the car and walked across the parking area to the entrance of the main classroom building. Once inside they parted company with a nod, and each made his way to his homeroom. Fifteen minutes later first period bell sounded, and another day of learning was under way.

It was not, however, for Jeff Bates. Try as he might, he simply could not concentrate on math or French or biology or any of the other subjects scheduled for that day. His head was too crowded with a host of tantalizing and torturing thoughts that were completely unrelated to his studies. Rather, they were directly related to just one thing: the list of fourteen names to be posted on the gym bulletin board after final class.

Would his name be one of the fourteen? The question hung in his mind like a brightly colored neon sign. One minute he didn't have the slightest doubt. But in the next minute his confidence would disintegrate, and he'd be overwhelmed by doubts. A dozen little things would come to mind: a poor showing during a certain practice session, a look of impatience Coach Doc Parks had given him when he missed a basket or let his man get away from him—each one insignificant by itself but collectively seeming to spell certain failure. Or so he thought until he was able to throw off the doubts and regain some of his confidence. On again, off again, he rode a mental merry-go-round.

And there was something else that did not help his mixed-up state of mind and the constant pangs of misery: what Paul had said about Frank Ames going after a college basketball scholarship. That had been Jeff's dream, too, of a way to obtain a college education. His parents had not left him very much—certainly not enough to see him through college.

So college was out for him, unless one of two things came to pass. One was that he make a name for himself in high-school basketball that would lead to college offers. Failing that he'd have to get a job after high school that would allow him to save enough in a couple of years to at least get started in some college—provided, of course, that Selective Service didn't get him first.

For Jeff, college via the basketball scholarship route

29

was a pretty obscure possibility right now. If he had made the team last year, he'd be on his way, maybe, like Frank Ames was now. But he hadn't made the team. That was a year lost in his efforts to win a college basketball scholarship. That left him only two seasons to make a name for himself. Or maybe it wasn't even that. If his name *wasn't* on that list, if he'd failed to make the team a second time. . . .

So it went as the hands of each classroom clock moved with agonizing slowness around the dial. Then, just before the final class of the day, his state of worry and impatience caused him to do something on the spur of the moment that was as stupid as it was embarrassing. He was walking along the hall toward his French class, when he suddenly spotted Frank Ames just ahead of him. It was then the crazy idea hit him, and, on an impulse, he quickened his pace and caught up with the other youth.

"Got a minute, Frank?" he asked.

Frank Ames, who was about the same height and weight as Jeff, had coal black hair and eyes, and a swarthy complexion. At the sound of Jeff's voice Frank turned his head, stopped walking, and regarded Jeff warily.

"What for?" he demanded.

"Nothing special," Jeff said offhandedly, already regretting his impulsive action. "I was just wondering— did Coach give you a look at the list he's posting?"

Ames's eyes tightened perceptibly. "Why should he?"

"Thought he might," Jeff said, feeling even more uncomfortable. "After all, it's a cinch you'll be on it, so I thought he might have let you know who the others are."

A faint gleam came into Ames's eyes, and the shadow of a grin passed across his lips.

"Meaning you, huh?"

Jeff swallowed a groan and nodded. "Meaning me. Did he?"

"Why ask me?" Ames countered, the gleam still in his eyes. "Bert Holland's captain this year. Or didn't you know? Ask him."

Jeff felt the red flood his cheeks but held his temper under control.

"When I saw you just now, the thought came to me, that's all," he said evenly. "Look, let's just forget it."

"Right. Forget it!" Ames snapped and walked away.

Jeff stared after the retreating figure as disgust and anger at himself boiled up within him. Presently he was able to smother his emotions and continue on his way to French class. An hour later the final bell sounded, and when he heard it an aching dryness came into his throat, and his heart started to pound against his ribs. Only a few minutes now, and he would know.

It was more than a few minutes, however. He returned to his homeroom to collect a couple of textbooks and papers he needed for homework that night, but he'd misplaced one of the papers, and it was some time before he found it. Snatching it out of its hiding place,

31

he hastened out the rear door of the building and over to the main doors of the half-million-dollar gymnasium. Paul Young was there, pacing impatiently.

"What the heck happened to you?" he exploded as Jeff came up. "I was just about to go in without you!"

"Couldn't find a chemistry paper. Sorry," Jeff told him. He took a deep breath and nodded at the double doors. "Okay?"

"What do you think I've been waiting for?" Paul bit off. "Let's go!"

They went inside, turned right, and headed for the bulletin board that was fastened to the wall just to the left of the door leading into the locker rooms. A group of some twenty youths was in front of the bulletin board, and it was all Jeff could do not to break into a mad run. He held himself in check, though, and, with Paul, walked over to the group and shouldered through it for a look at the list of names thumbtacked to the board.

A kind of dizziness swirled through Jeff, making it impossible for him to focus his eyes on the list of names. It passed in a second, however, and the printed names became legible. Bert Holland, the team's captain, headed the list, and next was Frank Ames. Paul Young's name was halfway down the list—and at the very bottom of the list was his own!

The sight of his name caused something to let go inside of him. It was as if a tight steel band around his chest had snapped loose. A vast sense of relief flooded through him, and a wild yell started up in his throat.

With a tremendous effort, he choked it back and simply stood there, staring at his name on the list and savoring the most wonderful moment of his life thus far. But suddenly the memory of last night's horrible nightmare came flooding back. Hardly realizing what he was doing, he stepped closer to the board, reached out a finger, and started counting the names on the list. They totaled fourteen, exactly.

"What was the idea of that?" he heard Paul ask.

Jeff turned to him, opened his mouth, and then closed it, with a shake of his head.

"Nothing. Skip it," he said and put out his hand. "Congratulations, pal!"

"You, too!" the other youth said, shaking his hand firmly. "But, like the man said, it's only the beginning. Right?"

"Right," Jeff echoed. "But right now I'll settle for that."

Paul grinned and started to say something, but he checked it as the door to the locker rooms swung open and Doc Parks stepped through.

3 *Down to Business*

THE COACH of the Bedford High School basketball team was not the kind of man who would stand out in a crowd, save for one thing—a shiny bald head. Beyond that, he possessed not one distinguishing feature that might set him apart from countless other men in their middle years.

Doc Parks was forty-five years old, five feet eleven inches tall, and of medium build. He was also a natural athlete. In high school he had set all kinds of records as a basketball player and had gone on to college to do more of the same. He was unanimously selected All-American in both his junior and senior years at Holy Cross and received half a dozen contract offers to play professional basketball. He finally signed with the Chicago Beavers, and much was written, speculating on the big boost he would give that team.

Unfortunately for Parks, it did not quite work out that way. He was every bit as much a scrapper with the Beavers as he had been at Holy Cross—even more as he gained pro experience—but he had two things going against him, and nothing in the world could change them: his height and his reach. They just weren't enough in the pro ranks, where a six-footer is practically a midget. At the end of a season with the Beavers, the handwriting on the wall was plain to see. Doc retired from professional basketball and turned to coaching as a way of making a living in the sport he loved.

Because he had always been able to get along well with younger people, Doc chose high-school basketball, and it proved to be a good choice. In a few short years he managed to build a name for himself as a coach who could put together winning basketball teams. Five years ago Bedford had hired him at a salary which was said to top that paid to any other high-school basketball coach in the state, and he had lost no time in earning his money.

Starting with a team that had finished last in the league the year before, he put together a team that

35

finished third. The next year the Bedford team finished second, and the third and fourth years Doc Parks's team went all the way—that is, almost all the way. Bedford won its league title both years and was invited to the State Tournament, but they were eliminated in their first game. And just last year, when it seemed certain that Bedford had another league winner, the flu struck a couple of key players, and they lost the league title-clinching game by a single point.

When Parks came through the locker-room door, the group in front of the bulletin board fell silent and turned to face him. He came to a stop before them, looked them all over for a moment, and nodded.

"All right," he said quietly. "You fellows on the list go suit up. We've got work to do. You other fellows—I want to thank you for coming out and giving it such a good try. I appreciate it, and I only wish I could keep you all on the squad. But I can't, and. . . ."

Jeff didn't hear what else the coach had to say. He and the other thirteen squad members were already crowding through the door into the dressing rooms. As Jeff took off his street clothes and put on his suit, his hands trembled slightly, and a butterfly or two fluttered around in the pit of his stomach. Every school day since the start of practice over three weeks ago, he had put on his suit with a desperate determination and hope that he would make the final cut. Well, now he *had* made the final cut, but, as Paul had noted, it was only the beginning. Now came the big test—the test to

see whether he was to be a bench warmer or a regular
player.

Ten minutes later the entire squad was out on the
court, shooting baskets to limber up. After some fifteen
minutes, Doc Parks blew his whistle and gathered them
around him.

"Well, away we go, fellows," he said when they
were all grouped in front of him. "Barring the unforeseen—and let's all keep our fingers crossed—
you're the ones who'll do the job—go all the way to the
league title, and *then* to the state championship."

He paused to nod and grin.

"That's right, the state championship," he repeated.
"This year we're going to take it. Now, I realize we
don't have Jones and Hicks with us anymore. They were
two of the best basketball men I've ever had the pleasure
of coaching. And I also realize that we've yet to be
tested in our first game against Alston High a week from
tomorrow night. But I've had a very good look at all
of you, and it's given me the feeling that this really is
going to be *our big year*. I'm not about to settle for anything less, so keep it in mind."

He paused again to smile and make a little gesture
with both hands.

"Okay, so much for that," he said. "Now, down to
serious business. We'll start with the same A and B
teams as yesterday. Let's go!"

After whacking his palms together, the coach picked
up a basketball and walked out to the center ring. Ten

of the group followed him out, five going to the north side of the jumping circle and five to the south side. Jeff was in the five that went to the north side, and being one of them today made him feel extra good. Three of the other four—Bert Holland, Frank Ames, and Steve Tate—had been members of last year's varsity five.

On the first day of the season's practice Doc Parks had announced to the sixty-odd youths assembled in the gym that every position on the team was wide open. Ability and performance were the two things he wanted, and whether he got them from a veteran of last year's squad or from a rookie was unimportant. Just the same, he had used Holland, Ames, and Tate as a nucleus for the new team and had concentrated his efforts on finding the two players best fitted to fill the vacant positions.

True, he had taken several long, hard looks at every youth trying out, but within a week he was able to see that Holland, Ames, and Tate were not going to be seriously challenged for their jobs. With that settled, he went looking for someone to take over Hicks's vacated forward slot and Jones's old guard position. Equally important, of course, was the development of a strong bench.

Parks looked for many things in a player, but, first of all, defensive ability. Doc was a strong believer in the theory that defense was eighty percent of basketball. He would often declare, "Give me a good defense and control of both boards, and I'll give you a winning team." Of course, he fully realized that it was good shooting that got points, but his first concern was never to find a sharpshooter around whom to build a team. On the contrary, Doc Parks was a dedicated team play coach, on both offense and defense. Just as he insisted that his players be able to drive an opponent to the baseline, harass the man with the ball, trap, switch off, stick close or play loose, and climb the boards on defense, so did he insist that they all be able to shoot with a fair amount of accuracy whenever they had the ball and the opportunity. In short, he demanded *team play* offense and defense, from the opening tap-off to the horn ending the game.

The reason Jeff felt so good now as he moved out to play guard on A team, alongside of Frank Ames, was that this was the fourth straight day he'd started the practice session at that position. Before then he'd taken turns starting with Paul and a fellow named Jack Bevins. But for four days, now, he had started and had not been taken out, except for breathers. Whether it meant something he wasn't at all sure, but his hopes were soaring. There was still a whole week to go until the season-opening Alston game.

As he took up his position and waited for the tap-off, he looked over B team and saw that it, too, was the same as yesterday's, Paul and Bevins at guard, and the front line made up of Phil Downs, Dan Logan, and Bill Carter. He took a second look at Jack Bevins. The chunky redhead was his man to guard. Bevins was fast and shifty and knew how to use his weight and strength

39

—and elbows—in close quarters under the basket. If he were more than just a fair shooter he'd be on the starting five. Another thing about Jack Bevins was that he was the only member of the entire squad, perhaps the only person in the whole school, who seemed to be on good terms with Frank Ames.

Doc Parks's whistle cut off Jeff's musing. He grabbed Bert Holland's tap and started upcourt fast, flipping across to Frank Ames. He got it right back, feinted left as Paul and Bevins moved in to cut him off, and then threaded the needle between them on a hard bounce pass to Holland, who had moved into the key. The tall pivot man took it cleanly, went up in a twisting jump, and flicked a jumper high off his finger-tips. The ball hit the rim and bounced high. Tearing in, Jeff climbed the boards to tip it in, but Bevins went up, too, giving him the hip, and slapped the ball away. Ames grabbed the ball before it could go over the baseline, ducked around Paul's waving arms, and made the lay-in.

Jeff didn't see the shot made, because he was picking himself up off the floor where Jack Bevins's hip play had dumped him. The air had been slammed out of his lungs, and he was a little groggy when Doc Parks whistled the ball dead and came over to him.

"You all right, Jeff?" Doc asked.

Jeff dragged some air into his lungs and nodded. "I'm okay, Coach," he said.

Parks gave him a second's appraisal, then signaled

40

for B team to bring out the ball. Jeff turned with the others and headed toward A team's end of the court; as he did he saw something that he didn't like. Frank Ames was grinning broadly at Bevins, who had dumped Jeff. The action puzzled him. This was the first time he'd seen usually unsmiling Frank Ames exhibit pleasure at another player's misfortune.

Why now, when he'd tangled with Bevins and lost? Did the final cut have something to do with it? Had Ames expected him not to make the cut and thus to increase Bevins's chances of getting picked for the vacant guard slot? Personally, Jeff thought that Paul was a much better player than Bevins, but maybe Ames didn't think so. And now that Jeff had made the cut, Ames was pleased to see Bevins make him look bad at the boards.

Maybe. But he spent only a couple of seconds thinking about it. B team brought the ball out, Paul and Jack Bevins working it up across the center line. The A team defense moved out to stop them from penetrating too close, and on a pass from Paul to Bevins, going down the right lane, Jeff moved out quickly to run him into the baseline. The redhead feinted a dribble around him and whipped the ball to Phil Downs, who had slid into the key. Jeff, alert to such a move, shot out his hand to deflect the pass, then gathered up the ball on the dead run. In a dazzling burst of speed, Paul came after him but wasn't quite fast enough. Jeff went all the way for an easy lay-up.

At that point Doc Parks blew the ball dead and proceeded to point out some mistakes that both teams were making. As Jeff listened he suddenly had the feeling that eyes were on him, and a quick turn of his head to the right confirmed the feeling. Frank Ames was looking at him, eyes hard, with an unmistakable frown of disapproval knitting his coal black brows. In a flash the frown disappeared, and the eyes switched to Doc Parks, but not before Jeff had seen them both and decided that Ames hadn't liked his stealing the ball from Jack Bevins.

Parks finished what he had to say and got the practice game going again. On their second try at bringing the ball out, B team, perhaps stung by some of the coach's comments, went at it with a vengeance. They fairly stormed down the court and worked the ball in close for a clean shot. The ball hit the rim and then caromed off the boards into the hands of Bert Holland, who had gone up high.

The Bedford captain came down with elbows out and body twisting and snapped the ball out to Steve Tate to begin a fast break. He immediately whipped the ball to Jeff, charging up the center, a good two steps in front of his man. Jeff took the lead pass and fed off to Ames, who had broken momentarily into the clear. He angled for the basket, but Jack Bevins zoomed up out of nowhere to get in front of Ames, and he whipped the ball back to Jeff. It was a real mustard pass, and Jeff almost couldn't hang on to it. He did, though, and

43

as Ames and Tate screened Bevins, he pushed it in for the score. When he turned to trot back upcourt, he saw Ames grin at Bevins.

"Nice try, Jack," Ames said. "Lucky basket for us, that's all."

The compliment surprised Jeff, because it was a rare thing when the uncommunicative Ames spoke words of praise even to a teammate, let alone an opposing player. He wondered if the comment had been made for his benefit, rather than Bevins's. Was that the way Ames was letting him know he'd rather have Jack Bevins in the other guard spot when the regular season started? It could have been, and the possibility made Jeff do a slow burn. Getting assigned to the starting five against Alston was going to be tough enough, without Ames taking advantage of any opportunity to make him look bad. And there would be many such opportunities.

After five more minutes of scrimmage, Doc Parks blew the whistle and made some lineup changes. One of them—to Jeff's keen disappointment—sent Jeff to the bench and switched Jack Bevins over from B team to play his vacated slot on A team.

4   *The Breaks of the Game*

THE DAY of the season's opening game between Bedford and Alston dawned crisp and clear, but by four o'clock in the afternoon a cloud cover had moved in. By five o'clock there was a light drizzle, by six o'clock it was really raining, and by seven there was a steady downpour from the black heavens.

The adverse weather, however, had little, if any, effect on the game's attendance. Bedford had always been a red-hot basketball city, and the season's opening game was one you just didn't miss, no matter what. And so, with still half an hour to go before the tap-off, the portable grandstands along the court sides and at the two ends were packed solidly, from top to bottom.

In the Bedford section of the locker rooms, all the players were suited up and sitting quietly on benches as Coach Parks delivered his pregame talk.

"You've got a fight on your hands tonight," he was saying. "Make no mistake about that! Their whole first string is back, so those of you who played against them last year know what to expect. They're rough and tough and have speed to burn. Don't hope they'll give you anything, because they won't. Incidentally, I understand they've been working hard on the fast break this year, so get back on defense fast, or you'll get caught. Better yet, don't give them the chance. Score, because that's the one sure way to defeat the fast break."

He paused for a moment, allowing time for his words to sink in, and then continued.

"Remember Kasco from last year?" he asked, looking at Frank Ames. When the youth nodded, Parks continued. "They say he's even better this year. Much faster on the feint and dribble and moving to either side. So watch him closely every second he has the ball."

Looking at Ames, Jeff saw him nod silently. A faint tint of red had come to his cheeks for a moment. Jeff had seen the Alston game last year, but he didn't remember anything special between Ames and Kasco, the big Alston guard. There must have been something, though, or Doc Parks would not have brought it up. And the momentary redness in Ames's face seemed to indicate that Kasco had the better of things, whatever they were.

"Well, that's all," Doc Parks said. "I think you can beat them, but it won't be easy. They'll fight you for everything, but I'm counting on you to do the same. And that's where I think we'll have the edge. Okay, let's go out and get the job done!"

With a nod the coach turned and headed for the dressing room door, but halfway there he checked himself and turned back.

"These men will start," he said, consulting the clipboard he carried in his hand. "Ames and Bevins at guard. Tate, Holland, and Allen in the front line."

Jeff felt a twinge of disappointment, but he wasn't surprised. In the final week of practice before the opening game, he'd seen less and less action at guard for A team. Mostly he blamed Frank Ames for the gradual dimming of his hopes of being one of the starting five. When he'd been paired with Ames at guard during practice, the swarthy-complexioned youth had given him a minimum of cooperation. Ames had taken advantage of every opportunity to make him look bad. But when Jack Bevins played with Ames, it had been completely different. Frank had cooperated one hundred percent and often set things up so that Bevins could rack up a score on a good-looking play. More than once Jeff had looked at Doc Parks to see if the coach was wise to what was going on, but if Doc was, he gave no evidence of it.

It hadn't all been Frank Ames's doing, however. Jeff himself was to blame for a good part of it, and he didn't try to think otherwise. Perhaps it was because suspense and tension had finally taken their toll. Maybe he'd tried too hard or had even taken too much for granted once he survived the final cut. It could have been a combination of all three, but, whatever it was, his play had suffered. He had missed shots he should have made with his eyes closed, he had let his man get away from him on more than just one or two occasions, and he had committed other obvious blunders during practice play.

No, he was not really surprised at not being in the starting lineup, but even so he was bitterly disappointed. That disappointment engulfed him like a dark cloud as he went out to the court with the others for the warm-up session and then took a seat on the bench beside Paul as Doc Parks huddled with his starting five.

A minute or so later the huddle broke up, and the Bedford Squad moved out onto the floor to shake hands with their opponents and take tap-off positions. Holland's inch of reach over the Alston center allowed him to tap to Ames, who dribbled a few steps and then whipped the ball across to Bevins. He got it back as he cut into the center lane, and he fed to Steve Tate. The Bedford forward almost lost the ball, but he managed to hang on to it, shake off the man guarding him, and pass across to Ames again. Frank went up

48

for a high pass to Bert Holland in the key. The Bedford captain spun around toward the basket and jumped, but his man went up with him, preventing a clean shot. In the last split second, Holland saw Ames tearing in on the right side of the basket and slammed the ball down at him. Ames caught it and took one more running step before making a carom shot off the backboard.

The Bedford section roared when their team drew first blood, but it didn't last long. Alston brought the ball out quickly, and it was obvious that they had come to play basketball. They were big and surprisingly fast, and they made full use of both qualities. Almost immediately they had the ball right under Bedford's basket. There Kasco, wearing the number 5 on his jersey, took it, spun away from Ames as though to pass out to a man in the right corner, but spun right back and hit a short jumper. Ames hacked him as he made the shot, and Kasco's foul try made it three points for Alston, instead of two.

Shortly after that, Alston made it five points, when Kasco stole the ball from Jack Bevins and went all the way alone for an easy lay-up. Bedford came roaring back but with no success. On a jumper from ten feet out, usually duck soup for him, Frank Ames was short. The ball hit the front of the rim with a dull *thunk* and caromed straight up. Colton, Alston's big center, came down with the ball and rifled it out to Kasco, who was already racing down the right sideline. Bedford dashed upcourt to check the fast break, but Alston had them

49

by a couple of steps. Jack Bevins did catch up with the man with the ball, but a two-on-one situation put him out of the picture. Kasco scored easily on a well-executed return feed.

Bedford brought the ball out for another try, and this time everything went as it should. On a play similar to the one on which he had drawn first blood, Ames scored two more points. For the next two minutes after that, there was no more scoring. Bedford was too closely guarded to get off a halfway decent shot, and three basket tries by Alston just barely missed dropping in.

With four minutes left in the first period, Alston suddenly caught fire and scored three goals while holding Bedford to a lone free throw. With the score thirteen to five against Bedford, Doc Parks called for time and huddled with his team. From where he sat with Paul, Jeff didn't hear what the coach told them, but it didn't seem to do much good. When play was resumed, Alston quickly scored from the corner and, after stealing the ball, were off again. Steve Tate made a spectacular save at the Bedford basket and gained possession of the ball.

His great defensive play seemed to fire up the team. They quickly scored on a driving lay-up by Hal Allen, and then, when a bad Alston pass gave them the ball again, Holland tallied another bucket with a beautiful shot from the corner. It looked as if Bedford was on its way when Tate stole the ball under his own basket and, teaming up with Allen, crisscrossed the ball the full length of the court and bombed it in for another couple of points for Bedford.

Alston then called for time to talk it over, and when they went back onto the court and brought the ball out, it was a different story. They scored twice in less than a minute to get back their eight-point spread and throttled Bedford's efforts to whittle it down again. The home team played hard in their attempt to come back, but not quite hard enough.

There was something else that Jeff noticed, and he wondered if Doc Parks saw it, too. In this game Frank Ames wasn't carrying part of Jack Bevins's load as he had in practice games. With that whirlwind Kasco on him constantly, Ames had all he could do to take care of himself. The result was that Bevins often got into hot water, and Ames was unable to help him out. It also seemed to Jeff that Ames was far off his peak form. Usually a picture-book player to watch, he simply didn't have it tonight. Kasco's constant harassing and lightninglike moves probably had a great deal to do with it. Ames was finding it almost impossible to break loose and go for the basket.

With a half minute remaining in the quarter, Doc Parks suddenly got up and came along the bench to Jeff and Paul and squatted down so that he could talk to them and still watch the play on the floor.

"You two go in for Ames and Bevins the second quarter," he said. He tapped Jeff's knee. "Kasco will be your man, and here's what I want you to do—" His attention was diverted as Holland went up for a shot,

51

but when it was batted away into Alston hands, he continued. "You've seen how Kasco can feint and dribble to either side."

"Yes," Jeff said. "And he's fast."

"Very fast," the coach agreed. "But have you noticed something else when he has the ball within shooting range?"

Jeff opened his mouth, then closed it and simply shook his head.

"He doesn't shoot when he goes right," Parks told him. "Only when he goes left. So don't let him suck you over when he goes right. Follow him, of course, but not too tight. Hang back half a step so that you'll be with him when he goes left. When he goes right, give him his head if you have to. But when he goes left, don't give him a thing. Stick like glue. Got it?"

Jeff nodded as the quarter ended. Parks left them to meet the team coming off the floor, and Jeff and Paul went over to report the second-quarter lineup change at the officials' table. When they joined the huddle, Ames and Bevins were sitting on the bench toweling their faces. Jeff glanced at Frank as he walked by, but if he expected to read anything from the expression on Ames's face, he was disappointed. Ames simply gave him a flat-eyed look and went on toweling his face.

As the teams took the court for the start of the second quarter, Jeff tried to swallow the sudden dryness from his mouth and throat. His nerves were stretched taut, and butterflies played tag in his stomach. He was playing his first basketball game for Bedford High School, and the jitters had him in their power. He knew that once the action got going he'd be able to shake them off. And he'd better, too! But at the moment he was in sort of a semihypnotic state, and each second seemed a minute. He glanced up at the section of seats where he knew his aunt would be sitting, but it was just a blur of faces. He glanced nervously at Paul as the official prepared to toss for the jump.

Paul scrambled to control the tap, raised the ball above his head, and looked for a loose man. Jeff had feinted to his right, and when the back-tracking Kasco came after him, he cut sharply toward the sideline. Paul shot a lead pass out to Jeff, who took it on the run and whipped it back over to Allen going straight for the key. Allen tried to work it in for a quick feed to Holland at the baseline but it was blocked off and, instead, slammed it to Steve Tate cutting for the basket, with a step on his man. Tate had too much momentum to recover, and his off-balance reverse lay-up sailed clear over the rim.

Jeff had followed to the baseline. He timed his leap perfectly, but big Kasco was there, too, and practically slammed the ball down Paul's throat and over the baseline, off Jeff's shoulder. With the throw-in from close under Alston's basket, the Bedford players put on a hurried press, hoping to force a mistake and get a quick goal. The press failed to unnerve the Alston guard, who delayed a second, then tossed in to a forward who had come back to help him out.

Maneuvering the ball skillfully with a series of short, quick passes, Alston worked it in close to the basket, but Bedford, applying the pressure, prevented them from setting up a clear shot. The ball came back out to Kasco, who drove to his left, past a pick from an Alston teammate. Jeff, sliding behind the pick, stayed right with him. Kasco reversed direction to his right, but Jeff remembered Doc Park's instructions and overplayed him to the left. When Kasco suddenly switched directions once more, this time to his left, Jeff was right in there close. When the Alston star released his twisting shot, Jeff was right there to bat it away. Bert Holland got to the loose ball first and flipped it over to Paul, who had shaken loose from his man and was starting upcourt. The Alston defender raced after him, but Paul had a three-step lead and scored easily. As Kasco headed upcourt to receive the toss-in, he gave Jeff a quick grin and a nod of his head.

"Nice block," he said.

"Thanks," Jeff said, noticing at the same time that the butterflies in his stomach had somehow settled.

Beginning with that moment, he was both completely relaxed and keenly alert to everything that was going on. True, he was unable to check Alston from storming back and making up for their lost basket. But, as play went along, it did help him to be at the right spot at the right time and make the right move.

Bedford suddenly got hot and put on a rally, Jeff contributing his full share of the effort. He scored four of the eight points that Bedford collected in a hurry, and his guarding of Kasco hindered the big man's efforts considerably.

With only two minutes to half time and Bedford within three points of Alston, Paul Young took a spill that knocked the wind out of him. Parks sent Frank Ames back in to replace Paul. No more than ten seconds after that, it happened.

An Alston shot was neatly batted down by Bert Holland, and there was a scramble for the loose ball. Jeff and Kasco went after it, and so did Frank Ames. It was Jeff who got his hands on the ball a half step ahead of Kasco. But, as he scooped it up on the dead run, Ames, trying to veer off, crashed into him. The impact jarred the ball from Jeff's grasp and knocked him to the floor, against Kasco's legs. Unable to keep his balance, the big Alston guard toppled down on top of him. Jeff felt white-hot pain streak up his right arm and into his brain, and then dark silence engulfed him.

5 Disappointing Setback

WHEN JEFF BATES opened his eyes he was in a hospital bed with his head elevated. His right arm was in a cast, from the knuckles to a point just above his elbow. There was no feeling of pain in his arm, but there was a dull ache on the right side of his head. When he explored with his left hand, he felt a good-sized lump under several layers of bandage.

"Well, young man, are you with us to stay this time?"

The sound of the voice drew his eyes toward the

foot of the bed, to a smiling middle-aged man wearing a doctor's white coat. Jeff tried to grasp the meaning of the words, but his aching head seemed to be filled with cotton.

"Stay?" he mumbled.

"You woke up a little while ago," the doctor said, "but you went right back to sleep. How do you feel now?"

This time the doctor's voice seemed to dispel the cottony sensation in Jeff's brain, and he understood.

"Okay, I guess," he said. He looked down at the cast and back at the doctor. "Where am I? What happened?"

"Bedford General Hospital," the doctor told him. "You had an accident in the basketball game. Do you remember?"

At that moment the memory suddenly came pouring back into his head. He nodded, then winced as the dull ache became a stab of pain.

"Yes, I do now," he said when the pain had gone away. "We were scrambling for a loose ball—" Jeff cut himself off as he caught sight of his aunt and Paul Young seated beside the bed. He grinned and started to nod, but stopped himself in time. "Hi," he said.

"Hi to you, too," his aunt said lightly. "Do you really feel all right, Jeff?"

"Sure," he told her. "The head aches a little bit— Hey, how'd we do?"

"We won," Paul said. "Only by two points, though.

It was a real battle, but Frank got hot in the last quarter, and that did it."

Jeff started to speak, but a chilling thought made him turn his eyes to the doctor. "My arm—is it bad?"

"You're a lucky young man," the doctor told him. "When they brought you here it looked like a concussion, but the X rays were negative. You'll have a mild headache for a day or two; that's all."

"I mean my *arm*," Jeff said, as the chill inside him increased. "I broke it, didn't I? Is it bad?"

"A compound fracture of the elbow," the doctor said. "A rather nasty break, but no cause for worry. There'll be no permanent damage."

"How . . . how long?" Jeff asked, finding it an effort to push the words out. "How long before it'll be okay?"

The doctor shook his head. "It's hard to tell exactly," he replied. "Perhaps in a couple of months we can remove the cast for good. Then, after a few weeks of prescribed exercises, your arm should be as good as new."

Two months! Jeff felt as though he had been kicked in the stomach. In two months most of the basketball season would be over—definitely over by the time he'd be in shape to play again. It would be two years, then, that he hadn't played. Last year he didn't make the final cut, and this year was out because of a lousy broken arm in the very first game. Tears began to sting his eyes, and he closed them tightly. He felt a hand take his and press hard, and heard his aunt's voice.

"Easy does it, Jeff. I know how you must feel, but let's be thankful it isn't worse. Your arm is going to be all right."

He opened his eyes and looked at her. "Yeah, that's really great, isn't it?" he said miserably.

"Your aunt is right, young man," the doctor spoke up. "You do have a lot to be thankful for. I'm sure you'd realize that, if you could see some of the more serious broken bone cases we've had here. You are lucky, no mistake about it." He paused. "Well, I'll drop in on you later."

With a nod, the doctor went out of the room, leaving the door open. After he had gone there was a long moment of silence. Then Jeff took a breath and sighed.

"Okay, I'm sorry," he said to no one in particular. "That's the way it is, and I'm stuck with it. If only—" He stopped and looked at Paul. "So Ames got hot, huh? Bevins, too?"

"Frank, yeah," Paul said, grinning. "But not Bevins. He was in a couple of times, but only when Doc Parks took me out for a breather."

Jeff smiled and momentarily forgot his troubles. "You, huh?" he exclaimed. "Hey, that's great! You're better than Bevins any day, and it's about time Parks caught on. How'd you do against Kasco? Did you get him for your man?"

"Let's change the subject," Paul said and laughed. "But, yes, twice, when Coach spelled Ames with Bevins and had me switch over to handle Kasco. That guy is fantastic! Talk about greased lightning—and tricky. Man, is he!"

"A good guy, too," Jeff said. "Another one like Kasco on the Alston team, and they'd have killed us in the first quarter."

"You're not kidding," Paul agreed. He suddenly snapped his fingers. "That reminds me," he said. "Got a message for you. Coach is coming around to see you tomorrow, but he asked me to tell you to hurry back, because Bedford can sure use you."

"Sure he did!" Jeff scoffed. "Heck, I didn't even play a full quarter."

"So what?" Paul snapped. "You showed plenty. I'm not kidding. You went over big with Coach. He was impressed by the way you blocked Kasco's try for that basket. I even heard him tell Ames to play Kasco the way *you'd* played him."

Jeff chuckled. "I bet Ames just loved that."

Paul grinned. "Well, he didn't look happy," he said. "But I guess you could say Frank won the game for us. If he hadn't got hot that last quarter, Alston would have taken it for sure." He stopped and frowned. "But if it hadn't been for my big feet, we'd probably have walked away with it."

"Huh?" Jeff grunted. "What do you mean?"

"When I tripped over my feet and took that spill, and Coach sent Ames back in," Paul said. "If Frank hadn't gone back in, you wouldn't have had that accident. You could have gone on to score a mess of points.

61

Now do you see what I mean?"

Jeff stared. "Of all the cockeyed thinking! Forget it!"

"Just the same," Paul said stubbornly, "I do feel responsible, in a way."

Jeff was about to comment further when a figure appeared in the doorway. It was a very tall, good-looking man in his middle thirties, with brown hair and eyes, an infectious smile, and a fine physique. "Hi!" he said. "How's it going?"

"Okay, thanks," Jeff said, struck with a feeling that he should recognize the stranger. But he didn't.

"Glad to hear that," the man said. "I saw the game tonight—that was a real nasty spill you took. I was visiting a friend up the hall, and I thought I'd stop by to see how you were. What about the arm?"

Jeff blinked as the man's identity suddenly came clear. "Of course!" he blurted out. "I recognize you! You're Ben Pinder, the star of the Baltimore Eagles. Right?"

The man laughed. "Right," he said. "But forget that star business. Everybody was tops on that club."

"I used to watch every Eagle game on TV," Jeff said. "You were terrific. You retired two years ago, didn't you?"

"Three years," Pinder corrected. "After eight years, I decided I'd just about had it. The young ones were beginning to run my legs off. So I decided I'd better call it quits."

Jeff remembered his other visitors and introduced his

aunt and Paul. Pinder, coming into the room, bowed to Kate Martin and shook hands with Paul. "You played a nice game tonight," he said. "Congratulations on winning."

"Thanks," Paul said, then added quickly, "It would have been a big one if Jeff hadn't been hurt."

"I'll buy that," Pinder said, looking back to Jeff. "I liked your style. You made some nice shots, and you're a good floorman, too. You handled Kasco nicely. He's a tough man."

"You can say that again!" Jeff exclaimed with a laugh. "But Coach Parks told me just what to do with Kasco."

"Maybe so—and Parks is a fine coach," Pinder said. "But if you didn't have the ability, you wouldn't have been able to carry out his instructions. And you certainly looked good from where I sat."

"Thanks," Jeff said, momentarily a little embarrassed. "Do you live in Bedford now, Mr. Pinder?"

"Temporarily," the tall man told him. "I work with your local YMCA."

"You mean you're coaching the Y kids in basketball, sir?" Paul spoke up.

"That's a part of it," Ben Pinder told him with a nod. "Shortly after I retired from pro basketball, I took the job of State Director of YMCA Athletics. I visit the various Y's to examine their existing athletic programs and recommend changes. Sometimes it takes only a week or two; other times it takes months. It depends on many things, but when I'm at a Y for any length of time, I

63

set up a basketball clinic for the kids."

"That's very interesting," Kate Martin said. "I take it you like working with young boys."

"Very much," Pinder said quickly. "I always have, for that matter." He grinned. "They're tomorrow's leaders, as the cliché goes."

"Quite so," Jeff's aunt said with a little laugh. "Anyway, I think it's a most commendable type of work for a man. But—" She stopped abruptly and shook her head. "No, that would be prying," she said.

"No, please," Pinder said quickly. "You were going to ask a question. Please do; I won't mind. I've been asked by many people, so go right ahead."

Kate Martin studied him a moment, a grin tugging at the corners of her mouth. "A mind reader, too?" she murmured. Then, letting the whole grin show, she said, "All right, prove it. What do you think I was going to ask you?"

"Sorry, but I'm afraid that's easy," Pinder said, returning her grin. "It's why I didn't take a full-time coaching job after I retired. Am I right?"

"Close enough," Kate Martin said with a laugh. "All right, why didn't you?"

Ben Pinder chuckled. "Well, it wasn't because I didn't receive any offers," he said. "I did, and a couple of them were quite tempting. But none was exactly the sort of job that I wanted. I decided to wait until the ideal job for me came along. That might not be for a few years, though, and even a retired pro basketball player has to eat. When the YMCA people approached me with their offer, I accepted. One reason is that it was nearest the kind of work I'd always been interested in. It still allows me plenty of freedom to seek out the kind of job I want most." He stopped and made a gesture with his hands. "Well, that's about enough of that," he said. "I've taken up too much of your time, and I must be getting along." He looked at Jeff questioningly. "Just how is your arm? How soon does the doctor think you can get back into action?"

The words jerked Jeff back to cold reality, and he experienced an aching emptiness. It was a moment before he could speak. "It's badly broken," he said heavily. "I'm out for the rest of the season."

"Say, that is tough! I'm terribly sorry," Pinder said. "But don't let it get you down too much. It's rotten, I know, but there's still next season. That's what you must force yourself to think about now. Next season—aim for it!"

"Yeah, sure," Jeff said in a completely dead voice. "Wait till next season. Oh, boy. . . ."

Ben Pinder frowned slightly and started to speak, but he said nothing. Instead he gave a smile and a wink that included Jeff, his aunt, and Paul. "Well, I'll be going," he said. "It's been a pleasure meeting all of you. Good night."

He turned and walked to the door, then stopped to look back at Jeff. "By the way, do you like to talk shop?" he asked. "Basketball?"

"What?" Jeff said gloomily. Then, fully understanding, he said quickly, "Yes, sure I do."

"Good. So do I," Pinder said, smiling. "So when you're up and around, why not stop by the Y sometime. We'll have a good old-fashioned bull session. Like to?"

"Sure! You bet!" Jeff said, his spirits rising slightly.

"A deal, then," Pinder said and went out the door.

He had hardly disappeared from view when a nurse came bustling into the room. "You'll have to leave now," she said to Jeff's aunt and Paul. "Time this young man went to sleep."

Ten minutes later, alone in the darkened hospital room, Jeff was trying to go to sleep, but the thoughts racing through his mind were making it very difficult.

6 *Looking Ahead*

JEFF REMAINED in Bedford General Hospital for almost a week before the doctor allowed him to go home. That made it two weeks before he was able to return to school. During the period of convalescence at home, he'd been able to keep up through daily visits by Paul Young, who brought him the needed books and homework assignments. During that time, also, Jeff had been able to climb up from the depths of despair, accept the facts, and get himself squared away. But it had not been an easy attitude for him to achieve.

After the final class on the day of his return to school, he went to the gym to watch basketball practice. During his absence, Bedford had won all of its league games. They were considered a sure bet to win the title and earn a berth at the State Tournament. Jeff had seen one of the home games with his aunt and had been very much impressed by the team's performance. They were nothing like the team that had just barely beaten Alston. Doc Parks had worked miracles since then. Bert Holland and Frank Ames were terrific, on both offense and defense. Jack Bevins was twice the player he'd been in practice games. Paul, along with every other member of the squad, was doing exceptionally well. Jeff had been pleased by what he had seen, but he had also longed to be right down there on the court alongside them.

His first visit to practice was an occasion. Everyone was glad to see him back in school, and they came over to talk to him and to express the wish that he could be with them and make an even better team. Frank Ames was the lone exception. He nodded curtly to Jeff and then ignored him. Ames's attitude, however, detracted in no way from the enjoyment of Jeff's visit. It was great to be back, even if only to watch.

He visited practice again the next afternoon, but things were a little different this time. There was no rush to greet him, no fuss made over him. Only Paul and a couple of others came over to sit and talk with him. Biggest of all was the difference inside himself. With the newness of his return worn off, cold truths dominated his thinking. He found it increasingly difficult to watch practice. He ached to be out there, a part of it, not just sitting and looking on. Not being able to play was almost more than he could stand, and before the practice was over, he left quietly. He didn't return.

On a Saturday, a couple of weeks later, Jeff was downtown and found himself in front of the YMCA. The sight of the building brought to mind Ben Pinder's invitation to drop by. On impulse, he went inside and was told that Pinder was downstairs in the gymnasium. Jeff made his way to the gym, but did not approach Pinder immediately. A swarm of young boys was on the basketball court, dribbling and shooting, with Pinder in the midst of them giving words of advice. Jeff waited for a break in the activity, but Pinder turned around and saw him and came over quickly. "Well, I was beginning to wonder!" the tall man said, shaking Jeff's left hand. "How are you, Jeff? How's everything?"

Jeff grinned. "Hello, Mr. Pinder. I'm surviving . . . I guess that's something."

Ben Pinder laughed and slapped him on the back. "That's good enough for starters," he said. "Just a minute, Jeff." He turned and blew the whistle hanging by a cord around his neck. When the kids stopped and gave him their attention, he yelled, "That's all for today, fellows. Put the balls away and report to Mr. Hicks at the pool as soon as you can."

"Look, I don't want to interrupt anything," Jeff said quickly.

"You're not, so forget it," Pinder told him. "Let's go up to my office, where we can be comfortable."

A few minutes later they were seated in a small but well-furnished office on the ground floor, with a window that looked out on the street. On the way up Pinder had gotten two bottles of Coke out of the machine. He raised his in a toast and smiled at Jeff. "Here's to our second meeting," he said. "Now tell me everything."

Jeff drank and wiped a drop from his chin with his handkerchief.

"What's to tell?" he said with a half grin. "I'm still lugging this load of plaster around. I've been back in school a couple of weeks now. And, oh, yes, I'm getting to be pretty good at eating with my left hand."

Pinder chuckled. "Can't stop progress, I always say. And your aunt—how is she?"

"Fine," Jeff told him. "She sure has been wonderful to me. Without her I guess I really would have gone off the deep end. She's been just great!"

"I can well imagine that," Pinder said with a smile. "Your aunt struck me as being a fine person. Tell me, have you seen any of Bedford's games?"

"I saw the Natick and Weston games," Jeff told him. "Bedford was terrific. We've really got a swell team. It looks like they're going to go all the way."

"Yes, it does," Pinder agreed. "I've seen most of the

games. Doc Parks has done a real top job with those fellows."

"He sure has," Jeff said. "Every guy on the squad has improved tremendously since . . . since I had my accident."

Pinder gave Jeff a quick look and then concentrated on having another drink of Coke. "Tell me," he said, lowering the bottle. "What about next year's team? What players on this year's squad will be lost through graduation?"

Jeff took a moment or two to run them over in his mind. "Well, we'll lose Bert Holland," he answered. "And Jack Bevins, too—he's a senior. So is Steve Tate. That's about it. I think all the others are juniors or sophomores."

"Three pretty good men," Pinder said with a nod. "But Doc will still have lots of fine material to work with. Incidentally, what are your plans?"

"Plans?" Jeff echoed with a frown.

"Plans for next season," Pinder pursued.

Jeff hunched a shoulder. "I'll try again," he said. "What else?"

Ben Pinder peered at him thoughtfully. "Meaning," he said, "you'll report the first day of practice and try again, eh? That it?"

"Yes, sure," Jeff said.

"And between now and first day of practice," Pinder asked, leaning forward, "what about that?"

"What about it?" Jeff was puzzled. "I don't think I

71

understand what you mean."

"Getting ready for next season," Pinder said. "What do you plan to do?"

Jeff frowned and absently drew the neck of the Coke bottle along the angle of his jaw.

"Get myself into good physical shape, I suppose," he said hesitantly. He tapped the bottle against the cast on his right arm. "But I've got to wait until I'm rid of this thing!"

"Why?"

Jeff started and blinked. *Why?* What do you mean?"

"Why wait?" Ben Pinder countered. "What's wrong with right now?"

Jeff stared, completely confused. "Are you kidding?" he gasped.

"Not a bit," Pinder said. He reached out and tapped Jeff's left arm. "Anything wrong with that?" he asked.

"No, it's okay," Jeff said. "But what's my left arm got to do with it?"

"Possibly a lot," the tall man said, "when next basketball season rolls around."

Jeff looked at him and shook his head. "I'm sorry, Mr. Pinder," he said, "but I don't know what you're talking about."

Pinder smiled. "I'm talking about starting *now* to prepare yourself for next season, Jeff. I agree that there isn't anything you can do with your right arm, but you do have a good left arm." He raised a hand as Jeff frowned and opened his mouth. "Let me ask you this—

72

would you like to start next season able to shoot left-handed as well as right-handed?"

Jeff understood and nodded vigorously.

"I'll say!" he exclaimed.

"Well, there you are," Ben Pinder said and spread his hands. "No need to wait for anything. You can start whenever you like."

"Hey, that would really be something!" Jeff breathed, his eyes shining. "I mean, if I *could* teach myself to shoot lefty."

"I don't see why you couldn't," Pinder said quietly. "Others have. Bob Cousy, the Boston Celtics' all-time great, did, when he broke his right arm as a boy. So why not you?"

"Yeah, so why *not* me?" Jeff murmured. His own enthusiasm was mounting.

"It would make you a better offensive player," Pinder told him, "particularly on lay-ups. It could almost double your scoring potential. A man who can go in for a lay-up from either side is a pretty difficult man to guard."

"You're right," Jeff said. He glanced out of the window and saw snowflakes drifting down onto the street. "Guess I'll have to wait awhile, though," he said. "I've got a basket nailed to the front of the garage, but the driveway's pretty slippery. I wouldn't want to take another spill on this arm."

"That's no problem," Pinder said quickly. "You can use our court. It's never in use between five and six. I'm

74

free then, and I could chase loose balls for you."

"Hey, that would be great, Mr. Pinder!" Jeff cried. "But I'm not a member of the Y, and I wouldn't want to take up any of your free time."

"Forget it," Pinder said and brushed the air with his hand. "Be my guest as often as you like. And as for taking up my free time, forget that, too. Tomorrow's Sunday. . . . How about Monday at five?"

"Great!" Jeff exclaimed. "Gosh, Mr. Pinder, I don't know how to thank you!"

"That's easy, too," Pinder said, smiling. "Just drop the 'mister' and call me Ben. All right?"

"Sure—Ben," Jeff said.

Sunday was the longest day Jeff had ever lived, but Monday finally did arrive, and when he reached the YMCA a minute before five, Ben Pinder was waiting for him. The former pro gave him a locker to use, and he quickly changed into the gear he'd brought along in his gym bag.

"A word before you start, Jeff," Pinder said when he was ready. "You'll find this tough—very tough—because of the limited use of your right hand. At first you'll get so discouraged you'll want to quit the whole thing. But that's the halfway point, and once you're past it you'll be on your way. All right? It's all yours."

As Pinder spoke the last word, he handed a ball to Jeff, who moved down to a position under the basket. He realized that it was going to be tough, and Pinder's

75

words echoed his own thoughts.

With Jeff unable to make much use of his right hand, the ball repeatedly rolled out of his left hand as he raised it to make a shot. And when he did get a shot away, the ball missed the basket and the backboard as well.

"Easy does it, Jeff," Pinder said when he rolled the ball back. "Try to relax and take your time. You're not going to get it today, so take your time."

Jeff clamped down on the angry words rising to his lips and tried again. And again . . . and again. He managed to hit the backboard twice. By six o'clock he seemed to be doing worse than when he'd first started. Despite Ben Pinder's many words of advice and encouragement, he didn't seem to make any improvement at all. It seemed hopeless!

"Well, that's enough for one day," Pinder said, ending the session. "We'll have another go at it tomorrow. All right?"

Jeff nodded, but didn't say anything. Pinder grinned. "I wasn't kidding, was I?"

"What?" Jeff murmured, only half hearing.

"About how rough it would be," Pinder said. "Not easy, is it?"

"Easy?" Jeff's frustration surged to the surface. "It's murder! It's—impossible!"

Ben Pinder regarded him soberly. "Do you want to quit?" he asked quietly.

By then Jeff had his feelings under control. He shook

his head. "No," he said grimly. "I'll get the hang of this if it kills me!"

"That's what I wanted to hear," Pinder said and slapped him on the back.

7 Opportunity Knocks

GRIMLY DETERMINED as Jeff was to learn to shoot with his left hand, there were many times during the next four days when, if Ben Pinder had not been there, he would have hurled the ball away and given up the whole crazy idea. Instead he stuck to it and slowly began to make progress. At Ben's suggestion, he'd worked on handling the ball naturally, with his fingertips, rather than palming it as he had done at first. Jeff found this to be a breakthrough, of sorts. He'd reached the halfway mark, as Pinder called it, and was starting to climb above.

Not that it was easy after that. It was one thing to hit the rim of the basket left-handed, and another to drop a shot down through. He didn't get that with any regularity for weeks. It took still longer to be able to do it from various angles and distances from the basket. But he did do a little better each day when he got together with Ben Pinder in the YMCA gym. The steady progress Jeff made was not the only thing that was pleasing to him.

He had become a close friend of the basketball star, and quite often he would have supper at the YMCA with Pinder and talk basketball. Ben was a veritable encyclopedia of basketball, not only on the game's history, great teams, and players, but on technical aspects, as well. He had many fascinating stories to tell about his own career, and his analyses of various play patterns were a basketball education in themselves. At his aunt's suggestion, Jeff invited Ben to dinner and an evening at their home. He accepted gladly, and it soon became a regular Friday night occasion.

Meanwhile the Bedford basketball team continued its winning ways. Jeff went to every home game, most times with his aunt and Ben Pinder. Doc Parks had performed more wonders with his squad, and they were knocking over the opposition with regularity. Frank Ames was outstanding, and he received much attention from the local sportswriters. Bert Holland was strong on the boards, and Hal Allen and Steve Tate were polished forwards. Jeff was especially amazed at how well Jack Bevins had come along.

One of the big reasons for Bedford's continuing success was the strength of the bench. When substitutions were necessary, Parks had only to send in Paul Young, Phil Downs, or Bill Carter. Bedford won its regionals and was one of the four high schools to qualify to compete in the State Tournament.

The tournament was held on a Friday and Saturday night at the huge Bedford Arena, which seated fifteen thousand people. Every seat was filled long before the first of the two Friday evening games. Bedford had drawn Winston High School as its opponent, and the game turned out to be a breeze for Bedford. They won 73–58 and could have piled up a higher score had Parks kept his best men in. He substituted often, once he saw how the game was going, and had his varsity five ride the bench for the entire fourth quarter.

The game for the state championship, however, was a different story. Bedford faced Hartford High, a school with almost twice Bedford's student enrollment, which put a team of giants on the floor. Bedford was equal to the challenge—almost. They battled Hartford up and down the court in a first half that saw the lead change six times. In the second half, Hartford slowly moved ahead to a three-point lead and managed to hang on to it long enough to win. Once again Doc Parks had been denied a state championship, but it was no disgrace for him or his team. They had given their best, but it hadn't been enough.

A few days before the tournament, the doctor removed Jeff's cast and assured him that the break had mended perfectly. That was a red-letter day for Jeff, because Ben Pinder had promised to teach him some other ball handling tricks, once he had the full use of his right arm. Knowing about the arm exercises the doctor had ordered, Pinder held off awhile, but Jeff didn't object to that. It was a relief to be rid of the cumbersome cast. And not only that; it greatly improved his left-hand shooting accuracy to be able to use his right hand a little when necessary.

At the end of the week, Pinder got down to business. First he gave Jeff pointers on how to feint the man guarding him into committing himself, then cut around him to the other side. Next came switching the ball to either hand as he went in from different sides for a lay-up. Playing the part of the defender, Pinder kept Jeff at it until he had the basic moves down pat. Then Pinder went on to the next item.

"Now for the behind-the-back dribble," he said. "Bouncing the ball from one hand to the other behind your back on the dead run. It's a very confusing move to the man guarding you. He loses sight of the ball for a second and is forced to guess which side you're going to. The biggest advantage to the dribbler, once he's mastered the technique, is that he needn't slow down or plant one foot to change direction. It's a very helpful offensive move but not recommended as routine procedure."

"Why not?" Jeff asked.

"Because it's merely a showboat technique unless it's used in the right circumstances," Pinder said. "And you look awfully stupid when it goes wrong. On certain occasions it can fool your man and get you into position to make a shot—particularly when you can shoot with either hand. Remember, though, its use is limited. Use it a lot and it will backfire. The opposition will be looking for it. Before you know it, another defender will sag off his man and steal the ball. So use it only when a situation really calls for it, never as a general thing. Okay? Here's how you do it. . . ."

Pinder demonstrated how it was done, in exaggerated slow motion at first, pointing out that it was essential that the player keep his body ahead of the ball to be able to catch the bounce with his other hand. After showing how it was done on the run, he had Jeff try. It required several practice sessions before Jeff was able to perform the trick ball maneuver to Pinder's complete satisfaction.

There were a number of sessions for Jeff to master other tricks of the game that Pinder taught him. Still more were spent practicing what he had learned in two-man competition with Pinder.

They were wonderful weeks for Jeff, but there were two things that constantly preyed upon his mind . . . the long wait he'd have until the start of the next basketball

season, and increasing eagerness to find out, through actual game competition, just how well he had learned his lessons. He tried to do something about the latter, asking around to see if there were any club or business basketball leagues that operated in the summer; there were none. Then, about a month before school let out, Ben Pinder helped him solve that problem.

It was a Friday night, and Pinder was again having supper with Jeff and his aunt. During the meal, Ben turned to Jeff and asked, "What are your plans for the summer vacation?"

Jeff replied with a shrug, "Same as last year, I guess. Stock boy at King's Supermarket. Haven't checked with them yet, but they'll always give me a job."

"I suppose they pay you pretty well, don't they?"

"I don't work full time," Jeff said. "The pay averages about forty-five dollars a week."

"Not bad money," Pinder said with a smile. "When I was your age, tops for a part-time summer job was thirty a week."

"Why'd you ask, Ben?" Jeff probed, suddenly curious.

The tall man looked as if he were going to brush the question aside, but he didn't. "Oh, in case you were looking for a summer job," he answered, "I had something that might have interested you. But the pay's considerably less than forty-five a week, so forget it."

"No, Ben," Kate Martin broke in before Jeff could speak. "What kind of a job was it?"

"Have you ever been upstate to Lake Mohawk?"

84

Pinder questioned in a tantalizing voice.

"Have I!" Jeff cried. "Lots of times. Boy, is that a swell spot!"

"Indeed, yes," his aunt said. "When I was a girl we had a cottage there. I've spent some glorious summers at Lake Mohawk."

"Did you know that the Bedford YMCA has a boys' camp there?" Pinder asked.

"No, I didn't," Kate Martin said. "But I haven't been up there for a long time."

"Wait a minute . . . I remember," Jeff said as Pinder was about to speak again. "There was an article about it in the paper a couple of years ago. Some rich guy left the Y the land, and they were going to build a summer camp on it."

"That's right," Pinder said. "His name was Felton, I think. Anyway, I drove up there last Sunday, and they certainly did a wonderful job—one of the finest summer camps for boys I've ever seen."

"The job you were talking about," Jeff said. "At the Y camp. Right?"

Pinder smiled. "Yes, as a matter of fact. A job as counselor. There'll be eighty boys there this summer. They sleep in tents—eight to a tent—and there'll be a counselor for each tent. One of my first jobs is to recruit ten counselors."

As he spoke Kate Martin gave him a questioning look. "You mean you'll be at the camp, Ben?"

"Yes," he told her. "That's why I went up there last

85

Sunday. They'd asked me to run it this summer, but I wanted to take a look at it before I accepted the job." He paused and grinned. "It took me all of one minute to decide to accept. It's a beautiful spot for a boys' camp."

Jeff looked at his aunt, and she read his mind. She gave him a little smile and a nod of her head.

"That counselor's job," he said, turning to Pinder, "sounds pretty interesting."

"It is," Ben said. "At least, I think so. I know I'd have jumped at that kind of a summer job if it had been offered to me when I was in my teens, if for no other reason than the basketball angle."

"Basketball?" Jeff echoed quickly. "What do you mean?"

"There'll be all kinds of athletic activities, of course," Pinder said, "but this summer the emphasis will be on basketball. A poll of the boys enrolled for this summer showed basketball to be the favorite sport. So I plan to set up a clinic for those who are really interested."

Jeff took a split second to glance at his aunt and see her nod again. "That's for me!" he said to Pinder. "The counselor's job, I mean. Is the offer still open?"

Ben Pinder looked from Jeff to his aunt and back again. "It was never closed," he said. "And I'd like to have you as one of the counselors. But there's the money part, Jeff. We pay a counselor a hundred dollars a month for the two-month camp season. Of course, you'll get bed, board, medical attention, and so on, but you'd still make more money at your supermarket job. Why don't you talk it over with your aunt and let me know in a couple of days?"

"I don't think there's anything to talk over," Jeff's aunt said, before Jeff could open his mouth. "After all —if you'll pardon the expression—money isn't everything."

"There you are, Ben; that settles it!" Jeff exulted. "What do I sign? What do I do?"

"I'll send you a form to fill out and sign," Pinder told him. "Have your doctor give you a physical and mail the results, along with the form, to me at the YMCA. A couple of days later you'll receive notification of acceptance and instructions on when to report."

"When will that be?" Jeff asked. "When does camp start?"

"It starts July first," Pinder said. "That's when the kids will arrive. The counselors and some other members of the operating staff will report on June twenty-ninth."

"I'll be there; count on it!" Jeff said, his excitement mounting. Then, as the thought came to him, he asked, "Have you signed up anybody else, Ben? Paul Young would like a job. I know he would."

"You're the first," Pinder told him, "but I intend to talk to Paul. His name is on a list I've made of Bedford High basketball players. I want to make up the whole counselor staff from that list if I can. I think that if everybody knows everybody else it makes for better cooperation and greater effectiveness."

"I agree," Kate Martin said. "I think it's a fine idea."

"Check. And what a break for us!" Jeff exclaimed. "Maybe we can split up and play practice games. It'd be a swell way to work into shape for next season!"

Pinder nodded. "I had that in mind, too," he said. "There'll be plenty of opportunity for that. And possibly a couple of games with Camp Ordway, on the other side of the lake. Their kids are in the same age group as ours, and I'm hoping to arrange a game or two with them—and between the two counselor staffs."

"Wow!" Jeff cried. He clapped his hands and vigorously rubbed them together. "Is this going to be a swell summer!"

His aunt laughed and nodded her head. "It certainly looks like it," she said. "Anybody for dessert?"

8 *Getting Settled*

At about ten o'clock on the morning of June 29, Jeff and Paul, in the battered Chevrolet, left Bedford for the ninety-mile drive to Lake Mohawk. They took their time, stopping for lunch on the way, and shortly before one o'clock they reached the crest of the first of the ring of hills that circled the lake. Paul pulled his car over to the side of the road and stopped.

"Boy, is that something!" he breathed. Jeff nodded. He had been to the lake many times, but it always gave him a thrill to come upon it suddenly and see all its majestic beauty. The lake was oval-shaped, about three miles long and a mile and a half across. In the rays of the sun, it looked like a huge sparkling jewel set in many shades of green. Because of the thick forest growth that swept down the hillsides to the water's edge, there was nothing man-made to be seen. It was like suddenly coming upon an area of nature completely untouched since the beginning of time.

"You can say that again," Jeff finally murmured.

When they reached the bottom of the incline, they saw the YMCA camp sign and the arrow pointing along a side road. Paul turned and drove through a tunnel of trees for a quarter of a mile before emerging onto open ground. They saw three more signs. The biggest one said YMCA CAMP. One said PARKING AREA, where there were a dozen or so parked cars. The one that said ADMINISTRATION BUILDING was in the shape of an arrow that pointed up a slight rise to a lodge.

"Shall we unload our gear or check in first?" Paul asked when he'd parked the car.

"Check in," Jeff said, getting out of the car. "No sense lugging it up there if we don't have to."

As they walked up the path to the lodge, they had a panoramic view of the camp, and what they saw pleased them. The camp was extremely well laid out with several narrow paths from one part of it to another. They were routed in a way that had minimized the removal of trees. In the center area there were two rows of five large-sized tents, and behind each row was a low-roofed wash-and-shower building. Off to one side and toward the shoreline was an outdoor basketball court, and close to it were three newly erected baskets for practice shooting when the court was occupied. Off to the other side were a softball diamond and an oval running track. There were also a volleyball court and a tennis court within easy reach of the two rows of tents. Near the Administration Building were a large mess hall, an assembly hall for rainy-day activities, and quarters for the camp's working crew. Finally, there was a long strip of sandy beach, complete with canoes, rowboats, and a diving raft.

"This I'll buy any time!" Paul commented as they reached the steps leading up to a wide veranda, which completely circled the lodge.

"You and me both!" Jeff echoed and started up the steps.

When he saw the eight other youths lounging in porch chairs, he instantly recognized every face. They were all members of last year's Bedford High basketball squad. But the sight of one face gave Jeff a shock— Frank Ames! For some reason it had never occurred to Jeff that Ames would be one of the counselor group. Not because Ben Pinder wouldn't offer him the job, but Ames was just not the type who ran with the pack. He was strictly a loner, and it was hard to believe that he'd be interested in a job as counselor at a boys' camp. But there he was. As their eyes met for an instant,

Ames's turned cold, and a thin smile stretched his lips.

The rest of the group came forward to greet the new arrivals. There was backslapping and small talk, but that was broken up quickly when Ben Pinder came out of the lodge. He came over to Jeff and Paul to say hello and shake hands, then addressed the whole group.

"Well, you're all here now, so welcome aboard, fellows," he said. "I have a few instructions for you, but they can wait. The thing now is to get you all settled. Go collect your gear and take it over to the tents. Each tent is marked with a counselor's name, but if any of you want to switch around, that's all right with me. The whole idea is comfort, convenience, and fun for all. If there's anything you don't like, let me know, and I'll see what can be done about it. There is a suggestion box just inside the lodge door. It's there for the campers, as well as staff members, and I'll be checking it every night. Use it when you want to, but, frankly, I hope I'll find it empty most of the time."

He paused to nod. "Okay, that's it for now. Go get settled and then report back up here, and I'll give you the grand tour of the camp."

Pinder went back inside the lodge, and the counselor group headed down the path to their cars. Each one collected his gear and lugged it over to the tents. Jeff and Paul found that their tents were side by side, which suited them fine. Two or three did not like the location of their tents and made swaps. Frank Ames swapped with Hal Allen, whose tent was next to Jack Bevins's.

Jeff and Paul were out in front of their tents when the swap was made, and they looked at each other.

"Looks like the loner has got himself a pal," Jeff grunted. "What do you know!"

"Yeah," Paul said. "They were friendly during the basketball season, but I didn't see them together after the season, so I figured it was temporary. Guess it wasn't."

"I was surprised to see Ames at the lodge just now," Jeff admitted. "Somehow I didn't think he'd be one of the counselors."

"Frank's changed," Paul said.

Jeff stared. "Changed? Since when? He sure looks like the same Frank Ames to me."

"Since the basketball season," Paul said. "Hadn't you noticed?"

"No," Jeff said. "But I hardly saw the guy the last three months of school, and I didn't talk with him even once. So how could I have noticed anything? How's he changed?"

Paul twisted his lips and shrugged. "Hard to explain," he said. "You have to talk to him to really see. I guess it's his attitude. Know what I mean?"

"No," Jeff said. "What *do* you mean?"

"Well, you know how he used to give you the frosty brush-off? Act like he couldn't care less whether you spoke to him or not?"

"Yeah, that I know," Jeff nodded.

"He's not like that anymore," Paul said. "Not so

93

much, anyway. It's—well, it's like he's suddenly got something going for him, and everything's okay. He's more relaxed, and not half as much on his guard as he used to be. Don't get me wrong—the guy hasn't become the buddy-buddy type. But he is more of a regular guy than he used to be."

"Well, I guess that's something," Jeff said. "The look he gave me up at the lodge wasn't his usual one. He even smiled. A kind of superior smile. He—"

"That's the word—superior!" Paul interrupted. "He's like that. Not stuck-up, but like he's got something you haven't got and knows it. Now do you know what I mean?"

"I guess so," Jeff replied. "What do you suppose changed him? Got any idea?"

Paul shook his head. "No, not really," he said. "But maybe being elected this year's team captain had something to do with it. And being most valuable player and being named for the state all-star team, too. That would make *any* guy feel pretty good."

"It would me!" Jeff said with a laugh. "If he has changed, that's great. I sure hope so."

"You'll see when you talk to him," Paul said with a nod and went back into his tent.

Later the ten counselors met Ben Pinder at the Administration Building and were taken on a tour of the camp. Seeing it all close up impressed Jeff even more. The YMCA people had done a splendid job, and any kid who didn't have the time of his life here had to have something wrong with him. As Jeff was thinking this, he glanced up and saw Jack Bevins, Frank Ames, and Pete Dixon, last year's second-string forward, walking along in front of him. Ames was in the middle and seemed to be monopolizing the conversation. He was doing a lot of talking, gesturing with both hands as he spoke.

Jeff couldn't hear what was being said, but apparently it was interesting to Dixon, who grinned and nodded repeatedly. Jack Bevins, on the other hand, was more interested in the tour and responded with only a word or two when Ames spoke directly to him. What interested Jeff most, though, was Ames's face, because he'd never before seen it as it was now—practically glowing. The coal black eyes seemed brighter, and the big smile—it still had something of a superior quality —often changed into a laugh. He decided that Paul must be right. Frank Ames certainly did seem to have changed.

When the tour was completed, it was close to supper-time, and after the evening mess, Pinder gathered the counselors together in the main room of the Administration Lodge and gave them a talk. He read off a list of camp rules and gave each counselor a copy. He outlined the counselors' daily duties and explained his rotation system. Working in pairs, they would supervise one kind of athletic activity one day and another kind the next day. Each counselor was responsible for the eight boys in his tent but wasn't to keep too tight a rein on them.

They were coming to the camp to have fun. At the same time, though, each counselor should be careful not to let his group get out of hand and become a nuisance to the other campers. After his talk, Pinder answered questions, and when there were no more to be answered, it was time to hit the sack.

The next day was one of hard work for both the administrative and counselor staffs. There were countless small jobs to be done to put everything in readiness for the official opening of camp on the following day. Everybody worked straight through from breakfast to supper. After the evening meal, with two hours of daylight still left, Jeff went over to the basketball court to practice shooting. He had tried to get Paul to go with him, but Paul had wanted to write a letter home.

After fifteen minutes of dribbling and shooting the ball, Jeff got the sudden feeling that somebody was watching him. He swung around quickly. Frank Ames had walked onto the court and was watching from a few yards away.

"Hi," Jeff greeted him.

Ames walked forward. He nodded his head at the ball in Jeff's hands. "Not bad," he said. "I hear you've been taking lessons."

Ames's smile—one of superiority—irked Jeff a little. So did the condescending tone of Ames's voice.

"Yeah, a few," Jeff said. "They help."

"Keep it up," Ames said easily. "It comes with a lot

of practice and hard work."

"Oh, I try, I try!" Jeff said, tight-lipped.

He dribbled the ball toward the basket, cut around to his right, and moving away from the basket, half turned and hooked a left-handed shot into the netting. He retrieved the loose ball, and, moving away from the basket to the left, he hooked one in with his right hand.

"Look, Ma, both hands!" he said with a laugh.

Ames also laughed and nodded. "Not bad at all," he said. "You keep that up and we just might be able to use you on the squad this season."

Jeff felt the blood rise to his cheeks, but he held back his anger. "Gee, thanks!" he said and nodded at the loose ball. "Take a couple of shots, why don't you?"

Ames shook his head and put his hands in his pockets. "Some other time," he said easily. "Too tired right now. But you go right ahead. See you around, Bates."

With that, Frank swung around and walked off the court. Jeff stared after him.

"Superior is right!" he muttered and went after the loose ball.

9 *Showboat Stuff*

OPENING DAY at the YMCA camp was a chain reaction headache for all in charge. Around midmorning the eighty young campers arrived like a swarm of eager locusts. They were hardly off the buses when they were all over the place, making necessary a general camp roundup so they could all be registered. When that was completed, there was the matter of assigning the boys to tents, and by the time they were all settled, or re-settled, in the tents of their choice, tempers were growing thin. Adding to the general confusion was the presence of a dozen or so parents with lists of suggestions, requests, or demands concerning the welfare of their individual children. They scurried about cornering anyone within reach and making general nuisances of themselves.

By late afternoon, though, things were in some semblance of order. The kids were settled in their tents, their personal effects were transferred from suitcases to the footlockers, and the last doting parent had driven away. The administrative and counselor staffs were able to breathe deeply and relax, knowing that all they had to face now were the inevitable cases of homesickness that would crop up during that first night.

It was a day or two before all had become adjusted to camp life and things were running smoothly. It was not until the start of the second week that the counselors really got down to business with their basketball playing. From five in the afternoon until evening mess every day there was an off-duty period for the counselor staff, and each member could spend it as he wished. At first a few, including Jeff and Paul, spent it on the basketball court, practicing shots and just fooling around. Each day a couple of the others joined them, and by the start of the second week, all ten counselors were making it a daily habit.

"How about some real action?" Ben Pinder suggested one day. "Choose up sides and play eight-minute

99

quarters. You'd probably be able to play a full game every day. It would be a lot more helpful to you than just messing around. I'd be glad to keep time and referee, if you'd like."

Pinder told Jeff and Frank Ames each to pick a team. The toss of a coin gave Ames the first choice. He picked Jack Bevins, and then Jeff picked Paul Young. Ames's three other choices were Hal Allen, Pete Dixon, and Bill Carter. Jeff's were Phil Downs, Dan Logan, and Jim Hall.

Jeff believed his to be the better team. Of course, Ames, Bevins, and Allen had played regularly for Bedford last year. Dixon and Carter had seen action in only a couple of games. But Paul had also played regularly, either at guard or forward, and Downs, Logan, and Hall, though they had seen only limited action, had handled themselves well. Dan Logan had spelled Bert Holland occasionally and, before the season was over, had developed into a fine floorman and a terror on rebounds. Another thing that appealed to Jeff was the fact that Jack Bevins, the only one who was not returning to Bedford this year, was on Ames's team. In the guard slots it would be Ames and Bevins against Paul and himself. Jeff believed he was going to enjoy that situation.

When the two teams had huddled and decided who was going to play where, Pinder tossed the ball for the tap-off, and the game was on. When Dan Logan and Pete Dixon sprang skyward, the tips of Logan's fingers were two inches higher, and he tapped the ball to Jeff, who took it across the center line before passing off to Paul. Paul fed off to Phil Downs, who had angled across into the key, and he whipped the ball to Jeff, cutting across from the right. With only Frank Ames between him and the basket, Jeff veered slightly right, pulling Ames over with him, then bounced the ball to his left hand as he cut sharply left for the basket and made a left-handed lay-up.

Jeff had noticed a faint, tolerant smile on Frank Ames's lips. But when Jeff outmaneuvered him and made the lay-up, the smile disappeared in a flash, and a look of startled anger filled Ames's face. Trotting back to his position, Jeff read the expression in Ames's face, and it made him feel good. Since that short meeting on the court the day before the camp opened, he hadn't exchanged a word with Ames, but he'd been very conscious of his presence. Though it wasn't exactly true, it had seemed that just about every time he looked around, he caught Ames looking at him with that newly acquired superior smile.

This was particularly so when the counselors started fooling around on the basketball court during their off-duty period. It would be after he'd shot a basket or tried out the behind-the-back dribble or some other court maneuver Ben Pinder had taught him. Always, or so it seemed, he'd see Ames and that confounded smile. It began to bug him, and, although he realized he was being childish to let such a trivial thing bother him, it

101

continued to do so. It made him feel good to wipe that smile off Ames's face and give him something else to think about.

Jack Bevins brought the ball in over the baseline, and Jeff forgot all about Frank Ames and concentrated on playing basketball. In that, he succeeded to his own satisfaction and to the astonishment of the others, who had last seen him play in Bedford's opening game against Alston last season. Jeff was all over the court and an almost constant threat to score. When Dan Logan took a bad spill and scraped his knee, which put an end to the game, Jeff's team was in front by twelve points.

That pleased Jeff because of his original belief that his was the better team. But what pleased him most of all was being able to prove to himself that he could properly execute, in an actual game, all the new techniques he had learned during those long months of practice. Now he *knew*. Now he possessed that essential confidence in himself. Now he had only to apply the polish that came with actual play.

After supper that evening he went for a walk with Paul, and they wound up on the beach, watching the huge full moon slide up over the crest of a hill. For some moments they watched in silence, and then Paul chuckled.

"What's funny about that?" Jeff wanted to know.

"Not the moon," Paul told him. "I was thinking about the game today. You really put it to Frank

Ames." He stopped to chuckle again and nod his head. "Boy, I never saw such a surprised guy in my life!"

Jeff shrugged. "Didn't notice, myself," he said absently.

"Everybody else did," Paul told him. "Whatever it was you were trying to prove, you sure did. A few times you really made Ames look stupid."

"Good," Jeff grunted, staring at the moon. "But I wasn't trying to prove anything. Not to Ames, anyway."

Paul stared at him. "Come off it!" he snorted. "You must have been. Seemed like you tangled with him every time you got the ball."

"So what?" Jeff countered. "He was my man, wasn't he? Naturally we tangled a lot. Same as you and Bevins, your man. Just happened that Ames and I tangled more, that's all. I wasn't trying to prove anything to him. He was just another guy in the game to me."

"Yeah?" Paul echoed a bit skeptically. "Then who were you trying to impress? Wait a minute; I get it! Ben Pinder, of course. And why not?"

Jeff started to speak but hesitated. "No, not really," he finally said. "I guess I did want to show Ben I could do all right, but that wasn't the big idea."

"What was?" Paul prompted, when Jeff didn't continue.

"*I* was," Jeff told him. "I mean, my whole idea in that game today was to find out if I really could do all the things Ben taught me—in actual competition, I mean. If you or anybody else had been my man, it would have

104

been the same. I just had to know."

Paul thought it over a moment and nodded. "Yeah, that makes sense," he conceded. "But the way it looked, nobody would have guessed it. Sure looked like you were out to clobber Frank."

"That wasn't it at all," Jeff said. "Well, maybe one time—that first basket I scored against him. Guess I did try to give it to him then. That screwy smile of his bugged me."

"Ah!" Paul breathed. "Then you *have* noticed how he's changed! I thought you would. When was it?"

"The day before camp opened," Jeff said. And then he went on to give a brief account of his meeting with Frank Ames on the basketball court. "Yes, he's changed," he finished up. "But I wouldn't call it much of an improvement. Too high and mighty for me."

"Can't say I care much for it myself," Paul agreed. "But I think I've guessed the reason for his change. All the publicity he got. It's gone to his head. He knows he's a somebody now, and he's showing it."

"He sure is!" Jeff agreed. "But as far as I'm concerned, nuts to him. I couldn't care less."

"Maybe you should care," Paul said slowly, after a pause.

Jeff stared. "Why? Give one reason."

Paul shook his head. "I don't mean it that way," he said. "I mean— Well, he wasn't smiling when Logan hurt his knee and we quit. He was fuming and looking real mean."

105

"So?" Jeff grunted.

Paul hunched a shoulder before he spoke. "So maybe nothing," he said. "But you know as well as I do that he's a tough one to figure. For all we know, he could have a mean streak in him a mile wide. Guys like that do something about it when they're really burned up. And Frank's burned up, all right. You see him at supper tonight? He hardly spoke a word to anybody."

"No, I don't remember looking at him," Jeff said. "But if he's really burned up, well, that's just tough. I still couldn't care less."

"Okay, okay," Paul said with a sigh. "All I'm trying to say is that it might be a good idea to kind of keep an eye on him, in case he might try to do something to pay you back. You never can tell, you know."

"What would he try to do?" Jeff asked.

"How should I know?" Paul replied with an edge to his voice. "I'm only saying it might be a good idea."

"All right, I'll keep an eye on him," Jeff replied. He took a last look at the moon, now partially hidden by a bank of clouds, and got to his feet. "Let's go see if the kids are getting ready for the sack," he said.

Paul groaned, and they walked back to the tents. As they reached them, Jeff caught sight of Ben Pinder walking up the path, heading toward the Administration Building.

"Be right back," Jeff said to Paul, and he set off up the path.

"Got a minute, Ben?" he asked when he had caught

106

up. "I'd like to talk with you."

Pinder stopped walking and turned to look at him. "Yes," he said quietly. "What do you want?"

Something in Ben's manner seemed odd to Jeff, but he dismissed the thought.

"I was wondering, Ben," he said. "What did you think about the game this afternoon?"

"Frankly, I was rather disappointed," Pinder said bluntly. "Disgusted might be a better word."

The words took all the wind out of Jeff's sails, and for a moment he was speechless.

"What?" he finally managed. "But—why?"

"I would think you could guess," Pinder said evenly. "Apparently, though, you've forgotten what I said about trick ball handling, how it was only for certain occasions when it would be a help, how repetition was only showing off, and how, eventually, it proved useless as an offensive tactic."

"No, Ben, I didn't forget!" Jeff exclaimed. "I honestly didn't. I—"

"Then why this afternoon?" Pinder wanted to know. "Was that for Frank Ames's benefit?"

Jeff groaned and thought of the talk he'd just had with Paul. "No, it wasn't at all!" he protested. "And I wasn't trying to show off, either, so help me. I've just been talking with Paul, and he thought the same, too. But I wasn't!"

Pinder gave him a skeptical look. "You're not saying it was for me, are you?" he asked. "That seems hardly likely, if you really didn't forget what I told you."

"I didn't forget," Jeff assured him again. "But that didn't have anything to do with this afternoon. Sure, I hoped you'd think I was doing all right with all the stuff you taught me, but that wasn't the main idea. The main idea was to find out for myself how well I could handle the ball. That pickup game was the first chance I've had to really test things out. Don't you see, Ben? A test game for me to see if I could do the things I'd learned in practice with you. And that's all I was thinking about when I was out there. Nothing else, Ben, and that's the truth!"

Pinder studied him closely for a moment and nodded. "All right, I'll buy that, Jeff," he said. "You've made your point, and I believe you. But let's have no repeats. Concentrate on straight basketball. Use the trick stuff sparingly, and only when it will definitely help the team. Otherwise, you'll soon lose the element of surprise, and your opponents will tie you in knots. There's another angle to it, too."

"What's that?" Jeff asked as Ben paused.

"Spectator reaction," the tall man said. "In general, sports fans don't care much for a show-off—that is, unless he possesses the skill and ability to deliver repeatedly. A fancy play looks fine when it works. But when it backfires it can make you look awful silly. Believe me, I know. Once the spectators get on you, you feel pretty small."

"Yeah, I bet you do," Jeff said. "Don't worry; I'll

watch it from now on. That's a promise. But—Ben?"

"Yes?"

Jeff hesitated and then took the plunge. "The game today. What *did* you think?" he said. "Did I do all right? Was there anything I was doing wrong? I'd really like to know, Ben."

"You did pretty well," Pinder told him. "Especially the behind-the-back dribble. No, I can't say that I saw anything that a little more practice won't smooth out. Only, as I said, don't make it a habit."

"You've got my promise," Jeff reminded him.

Pinder smiled and gave him a slap on the arm. "I know, and that's good enough for me," he said. "Well, it's close to sack time. Good night, Jeff."

"Good night, Ben," Jeff said, and he went back down the path feeling subdued but still pretty good deep inside.

10 A Stern Warning

A STEADY RAIN the next day washed out any outdoor activity, but the day after that dawned bright and clear, and the camp resumed its normal routine. Dan Logan's scraped knee was better, and when the counselor off-duty period rolled around, all ten of them showed up at the basketball court. So did Ben Pinder, ready to officiate another pickup game. A suggestion by Pinder that they choose up sides again was turned down by Frank Ames and the members of his team.

They wanted revenge and were primed to get it.

Ames, in particular, was most insistent that they team up as they had for the first game. There was no tolerant or superior smile on his face today. Nor had there been the few times Jeff had seen him yesterday. It was as though Ames had changed again, back to his former image—that of a loner, suspicious, wary, and quiet.

Once the pickup game got under way, one thing became quite evident, at least to Jeff. The other team had its eyes on him, and they were eager to give him the business if he attempted a repeat performance of the previous game. He made no such attempt. Ben Pinder's words of warning were not forgotten. He restricted himself to playing straight, hard basketball, going to the trick play only rarely and when necessary. That way an element of surprise kept the defense against him off-balance most of the time. The defense, not knowing what to look for, often gave him the opportunity to pass to a teammate for a scoring shot. And as play went along, Jeff realized more and more the wisdom of Ben Pinder's words. Having ability with the tricky stuff, but saving it for the right occasion, resulted in his team's scoring repeatedly.

There was something else that became evident to Jeff. Frank Ames was out to get even with him. Ames wasn't openly resorting to dirty play, but when he had the chance to inflict a little bodily punishment, he was quick to take advantage of it. Once it was a seemingly

111

accidental trip during a fast break that sent Jeff sprawling. Other times it was when the two of them were battling at the board for possession of the ball. Whenever Ames went up first and grabbed the rebound, he would come down with feet and elbows wide. There was nothing wrong with that, of course. It was a prescribed way to come down with a rebound to get some maneuvering room. But, more often than not, Ames managed to come down hard on Jeff's instep or catch him in the ribs or stomach with a flying elbow.

The first couple of times, Jeff thought it was purely accidental—one of those things that happen in a hectic battle under the board. But when Ames continued his subtle dirty tactics, Jeff knew there was nothing accidental about it. Once convinced, Jeff set out to put a stop to it. When he got the chance he gave Ames a taste of his own medicine, and, after a few doses of it, Ames got the point. But that night when Jeff went to bed he had some bruises and aches to remind him of the pickup game. His team had won, 68–62.

If Ben Pinder noticed the bit of byplay between Jeff and Frank Ames, he made no mention of it. The next day he suggested again that they choose up different sides. This time he put stress on the advisability of doing so. He pointed out the fact that, with the exception of Jack Bevins, they would all probably be playing for Bedford High School, come basketball season, and the better they knew each other's style of play, the better it would be for everybody.

They all saw the logic of that, and from then on they switched lineups around each day.

As days passed, the playing ability of the group progressed steadily. They all had played under Doc Parks and were familiar with the Bedford coach's offensive and defensive patterns. They got some good practice running them off against each other. Ben Pinder suggested that and had a couple of other ideas that added to the interest and value of the daily pickup games. He also did some individual coaching, pointing out flaws and the way to correct them, and offering tips here and there that helped.

The daily pickup games quickly took on all the aspects of a basketball squad in serious preparation for the opening of a new season. They all enjoyed it thoroughly, but there were a few times when it appeared that Frank Ames resented Pinder's close personal attention to Jeff. There was one thing Jeff was sure of: Ames's increasing hostility toward him.

Since that one game in which they'd tangled under the boards and Jeff had returned Ames's medicine in kind, there had been no further overt acts of warfare. A few times Ames had seemed bent on roughing him up when they were in close quarters, but those times really could have been accidental. There had been other times when Ames could have let him have it but didn't. Ames's growing hostility had not been exemplified so much by his actions as by his attitudes and manners.

For one thing, Ames resumed his habit of cutting

113

Jeff cold and ignoring him. Whenever they were on the same team, Ames gave him only the bare minimum of cooperation, often leaving him in an impossible situation. Ames seemed to take great delight in Jeff's making a misplay that drew a disapproving comment from Ben Pinder. Whenever Ames caught Jeff looking at him, he returned the look with a sneering twist of the lips and icy eyes. At first Jeff wondered if it could be jealousy, but that just didn't make sense. He had, with Ben Pinder's help, become a greatly improved basketball player, but he knew he was not yet in Frank Ames's class. Sooner or later, possibly, but not now. And he felt quite sure that Ames knew that as well as he did.

Something was building inside Frank Ames, like the beginning of a volcanic eruption. Jeff could not rid himself of the feeling that at any moment the lid was going to blow sky-high. He soon discovered just how right he was.

One evening after supper he was walking along the row of tents on his way to the beach. As he passed Ames's tent, he heard an angry shout.

"Get out of there, kid!"

Jeff turned and saw Ames swing at one of the younger boys with the back of his hand. "Frank!" he shouted. "Take it easy! You can't do that!"

Ames, who had his back to the opening of the tent, spun around and charged angrily outside.

"You giving me orders, punk?" he blazed, coming to a stop in front of Jeff.

114

"Just some advice!" Jeff snapped, holding his temper. "Are you out of your mind? You can get in big trouble hitting one of the kids. You should know better than that."

"I can, huh?" Ames rasped. "And you'd like that, wouldn't you?"

"Don't be a dope!" Jeff retorted. "I couldn't care less what happens to you. I simply said—"

"I heard what you said!" Ames cut him off. "And I couldn't care less, either. So go on! Go on and tell Daddy Pinder. You're his little boy, aren't you?"

Jeff felt the hot blood rush to his cheeks, but held himself back. "What's that supposed to mean?" he asked as evenly as he could.

"What do you think?" Ames shot back. "You're his pet. Anybody can see that. What's he give you when you turn in some guy for breaking a rule? An extra bar of candy?"

Jeff forced himself to take a deep breath and let it out slowly. "Ames, you're really sick," he said finally in disgust. "What's bugging you, anyway? Me?"

"You?" Ames sneered. "I couldn't be bothered with you—or a dozen like you!"

Jeff opened his mouth, but a sudden voice behind him closed it.

"What's going on here, fellows?"

They swung around to see Ben Pinder just a few feet from them.

"Oh, hi, Ben," Jeff said quickly. "Nothing's going on.

115

We were just having a . . . discussion. About nothing."

"Yeah. About nothing," Ames echoed.

Pinder looked from one to the other, but before he could speak a voice came from the tent.

"It was so something, Mr. Pinder! He hit me!"

The three of them turned around to see the small boy standing in the tent opening. Pinder beckoned the boy over and squatted down in front of him.

"Who did, son?" he asked quietly.

"He did," the boy said, pointing at Ames.

Pinder twisted his head up to look at Ames. "Is that true?" he asked.

Ames grimaced and waved at the air with one hand. "Aw, I didn't hit him," he scoffed. "Just gave him a little cuff when I caught him in my footlocker. Didn't hurt him any."

"What were you doing in Mr. Ames's footlocker?" Pinder asked, looking back to the boy.

"Nothing, Mr. Pinder," was the instant reply. "Just looking. I wasn't going to steal anything. Honest I wasn't!"

Pinder studied the young face a moment and nodded. "I believe you," he said. "What's your name, son?"

"Jimmy Bannon, sir."

"Tell me, Jimmy," Pinder said, putting a hand on the boy's shoulder, "would you like somebody to open *your* footlocker and go through the things inside—your personal belongings?"

"I didn't *open* his footlocker," the boy said. "It was

116

open. I just looked inside, that's all."

"You just looked inside, eh?" Pinder said, holding the boy's eyes. "You didn't touch anything?"

"He was fooling with my camera when I caught him," Ames snapped before the boy could answer.

"I was not!" the boy cried spiritedly. "I was only looking to see if it was the same as mine. And I was putting it back when you hit me!"

"I didn't hit you!" Ames rasped. "Stop lying and—"

"Never mind that, Ames!" Pinder stopped him, not turning his head to look up. Instead he spoke slowly to the boy. "Look, Jimmy, you know about the honor system we have here in camp, don't you?"

"Sure," the youngster said with a nod. Then he added quickly, "But I wasn't going to steal it!"

"I know you weren't," Pinder told him. "But the honor system means more than just that we shouldn't steal from our camp mates. It also means that every camper should respect the rights of all the other campers. This means not using or even touching something that belongs to somebody else, without his permission. Do you see what I mean?"

"I guess so," Jimmy said, nodding.

"Good boy," Pinder said and smiled. "Well, I guess that takes care of that. You just forgot for a moment, and you're sorry. But you're not going to do anything like that again—right, Jimmy?"

"I won't, Mr. Pinder," the boy promised. Then he added, "It wasn't like my camera, anyway. Mine's better. It's a more expensive one."

"Mr. Ames is sorry he lost his temper with you," Pinder said, straightening up. "Aren't you, Mr. Ames?"

Frank Ames colored, and rebellion showed in his dark eyes. But he wilted quickly under Pinder's steady stare.

"Sorry, kid," he grunted at the boy. "Forget it."

"There you are, Jimmy," Pinder said, giving the boy a pat on the back. "Everything's settled. Now you'd better get back in your tent. Close to lights-out."

As the boy turned and went back into his tent, Pinder jerked his head at Jeff and Ames and walked a few steps along the tent row. When he was about three tents away from Jimmy's, he stopped and looked hard at Frank Ames.

"That was pretty dumb of you," he said, tight-lipped. "About as stupid as you can get. If you'd hurt that boy in any way, his parents could have hung us sky-high with damage suits. You realize that?"

"I said I was sorry," Ames muttered sullenly.

"You'd better be," Pinder said evenly. "From now on you use your head and watch your step, Ames. If that happens again, *or anything like it,* you'll be on your way home before you know what hit you. Do I make myself clear?"

"Yeah, I get you," Ames grunted, not looking at him.

"See that you don't forget!" Pinder snapped.

He turned abruptly and walked away, leaving Jeff and Ames standing there. Jeff started to speak, stopped, then tried again. It was difficult.

"Well . . . see you around, Frank," he said casually.

Frank Ames glared. "Don't bother!" he snarled and swung away to go back to his own tent.

11 Blowup

WHEN JEFF WOKE UP the next morning, it was drizzling again, and it kept up all that day and most of the next. It was not until the third day that outdoor activities were resumed, and when the counselors got together for their daily late-afternoon session, Ben Pinder had some news.

"Camp Ordway phoned me last night," he told them. "They invited me to bring the kids over next Saturday for a game with their kids. They also invited you boys for a game with their counselors. I accepted for the kids, but I said I'd talk it over with you and let them know tonight."

"What's to talk over?" Dan Logan wanted to know. "Sure, we'll play them!"

Pinder smiled faintly. "I said I was pretty sure you'd like to play their team, but it was really your decision. You see, I found out something I didn't know when I first got in touch with them. . . ."

"What was that?" Jeff asked when Pinder didn't continue.

"Ordway's entire counselor staff is made up of college men," Pinder said. "Two or three freshmen, but the others all sophomores, and with two years of college basketball experience. Now, personally, I think you fellows could give them a pretty good game, but it's for you to decide. Of course, there won't really be anything at stake; it'll be just a fun game. But you fellows may have second thoughts about going up against that kind of competition. Anyway, it's up to you."

"I say let's play them!" Paul Young called out almost before Pinder's words were finished. "What the heck, it'll be good experience."

The others instantly seconded Paul's suggestion, and Pinder held up his hands.

"Okay, okay!" He quieted them down. "I thought you'd see it that way. Fair enough, then. I'll tell Ordway tonight. Now, let's start getting ready for them!"

The prospect of a game with the Camp Ordway

counselors added spirit to the practice session that day. Everybody seemed to put out with a little something extra. Not that there had been much lagging before then, but the other practice games had been played with nothing to look forward to but more of the same. So, naturally, there hadn't been any abundance of do-or-die efforts. A game with another camp made all the difference, and they all concentrated on the job at hand.

The one who seemed to apply himself the most was Frank Ames, which was surprising to Jeff. During the last week or so, it had seemed to Jeff that Ames was losing interest in the daily sessions. He still played well, but not as he had at the start, and certainly not as he'd played for Bedford last season. Often he seemed preoccupied with something other than what he was doing. And, if anything, the incident with the younger boy had caused Ames to draw even further into his shell.

During the last two days of rain, Jeff had seen very little of him, but Ames was in a scowling, brooding mood, and signs of inner turmoil were visible. Jeff had not expected Ames to show up for today's practice game. He had, however, and, what's more, was working hard in preparation for the Ordway game. It surprised Jeff, but it also pleased him, because with Frank Ames at his best the team was sure to give a much better account of itself.

The YMCA counselors had four days before the Camp Ordway game, and Pinder drilled them hard during each of the practice sessions. Rather than picking

123

a first and second team, he mixed the lineups each day and drilled them individually instead of as team units. Although he didn't mention it again, he regarded the Ordway game as strictly for fun. He wanted to win, if possible, but not by keeping his best men in while the others sat the bench. Win or lose, they would all have an equal chance to play.

Saturday's weather was perfect, and shortly after lunch all those making the trip boarded the two camp buses for the trip around the lake. Camp Ordway gave them a rousing welcome, and after a short preliminary ceremony, the two younger teams got going with their game.

It proved to be an exciting game, though it couldn't exactly be called basketball at its best. But, what the youngsters lacked in skill and technique, they more than made up for in exuberance. Pinder had selected fifteen kids to make up the YMCA squad, and he gave them all a chance to play. The Ordway coach did the same with his group, and so there was an almost continuous parade of substitutions. When it was all over, the YMCA kids had won, 22–19.

Fifteen minutes later the two counselor teams took the court. Pinder named Jeff and Jack Bevins as the guards, and Hal Allen, Dan Logan, and Jim Hall as the front line—five pretty good basketball players. But they looked like midgets compared to the Camp Ordway squad, who were giants, and during the short warm-up period, it was plain that they were just as fast and

124

coordinated as they were big and strong.

When Ben Pinder named Bevins to start in a guard slot with him, Jeff was surprised. Ames was not only surprised; he was angered, as well. A deep flush came to his cheeks, and his dark eyes smoldered. What reason, if any, Pinder had for not starting Ames, Jeff had no idea, and he didn't bother guessing as he went out onto the court and shook hands with the smiling blond giant who would be his man.

Minutes later the ball was tossed for the tap-off. Ordway got the ball, promptly went to work, and scored. They scored again twenty seconds later, when Bevins muffed a pass and the ball went out-of-bounds. For the first two minutes of the game, it was all Ordway, as the big men racked up twelve points to only a single point for YMCA on a foul shot by Jeff. After that point, though, the YMCA team seemed to loosen up and find itself. Dan Logan hit for two on a jumper from ten feet out, and Jeff took the ball off a pick and laid it up for another two points. Ordway thundered back to score, and then Logan hit again; seconds later Hal Allen went up on a rebound to tip the ball in.

The YMCA rally, though, was short-lived. Ordway scored three times in rapid succession, and Pinder made his first substitutions. He sent Paul and Frank Ames in for Jeff and Jack Bevins, but he kept the front line as it was.

Jeff was glad to take a breather. The big blond Ordway guard had been murder. Guarding him had

125

been like trying to guard a runaway freight train. And working the ball against him was like working against a man with twenty waving arms instead of only two.

As he sat on the bench, mopping his face and watching the play, Jeff saw that Frank Ames was having the same kind of trouble. In fact, it looked to him as if Ames was having even more trouble with the big guard. Twice the Ordway player stole the ball from Ames, and several times he blocked what should have been scoring shots. Jeff noticed something else about Ames. He definitely wasn't playing the kind of game he had been playing during the four practice sessions. He did score a couple of baskets, but both were easy plays resulting from defense lapses. The rest of the time he was wild and uncontrolled.

The inevitable was bound to happen, and it did; in the space of two minutes, Ames was twice whistled for a foul. Right after the second foul, Pinder sent Jeff back in for Ames and substituted the entire front line.

Ordway was leading by sixteen points, and their coach sent in a whole new team. No doubt it was a gesture of good sportsmanship on the part of the Ordway coach, but it did nothing to alter the game in any way. The second team was nearly as good as the first team. Jeff's new man, though, was not so skilled a player as the big blonde, and not so big and fast. Jeff came pretty close to holding his own in their man-to-man

126

battle. Three times he broke loose from the Ordway guard and scored. Twice, when the right opportunity presented itself, he successfully worked the behind-the-back dribble. When there were two minutes to go in the half, Pinder gave him another breather, and he was secretly glad to get it. Ames went in for him, and Jeff had hardly sat down when Ames was whistled for his third personal foul. Jeff saw the look of annoyance that showed briefly on Ben Pinder's face, but Ames remained in the game. And he did score once before the half ended, with Ordway out in front, 48–27.

During the half-time period, which both teams spent sprawled on the grass at the sides of the court, Ben Pinder pointed out a few things that would improve team play. Just before the second half started, Jeff saw Pinder take Frank Ames to one side and say something. He couldn't hear what the words were, but he could tell from Ames's darkening face that he did not like what he heard.

The YMCA front line at the start of the second half was Downs, Logan, and Hall, with Jeff and Ames at the guard spots. They got the ball on the tap-off and scored first on a high shot by Logan from the right corner. Ordway came right back to score, then tallied again, when their big blond guard stole the ball from Ames and charged for the basket to pop it in.

Having the ball stolen from him upset Frank. A minute later, when the big blond had the ball under the YMCA basket, Ames charged in recklessly in a wild

127

effort to steal the ball but succeeded only in hacking the Ordway player as he went up for a shot. With four fouls on him, Ames was replaced by Bevins. Sulking, Ames took his time walking off the court and angrily batted away a towel somebody on the bench tossed to him.

When play was resumed, Ordway put on a blazing attack that netted them three baskets in the space of only a minute. Then, on a spectacular steal, Jeff went all the way to get one of the baskets back. Twenty seconds later Dan Logan hit with a beautiful twenty-foot jump shot, and it began to look as if the YMCA team had found a scoring formula. However, Ordway quickly smothered the rally attempt and proceeded to widen their lead by another four points. With two minutes remaining in the third quarter, Pinder sent Ames back in to replace Jeff and made a couple of other substitutions. But that didn't change the complexion of the game. Ordway scored two more baskets. With only five seconds left in the third quarter, Frank Ames committed his fifth foul, putting him out of the game.

Pretty well exhausted, but still determined to give battle with everything they had against a much bigger and stronger team, the YMCA group tried their level best in the fourth quarter. Jeff scored, and so did Dan Logan, but Ordway's second team, obviously not really putting on the heat, racked up four baskets for a game-ending total of 78 to YMCA's 52.

"No complaints at all, fellows," Ben Pinder said to the players when they gathered at the bench. "Believe me, you did a whole lot better than I thought you would. So don't feel bad about a thing. You did all right."

Shortly after that, the Ordway players came over to shake hands and speak words of praise for the serious battle YMCA had put up. The big blond guard and one or two others had special praise for Jeff's playing. That made him feel pretty good, but the pleasure was dampened a little when he happened to glance at Frank Ames and saw the sullen anger in his eyes and the ugly twist of his lips. Ames just hadn't had a good game, and Jeff found that he couldn't help but feel a little sorry for him.

On the bus ride back to camp, Frank Ames sat by himself, with his head turned to the window. The corners of his mouth were pulled down, and his eyes were fixed, unseeing, on the passing scenery. Once or twice Jeff felt an impulse to go over and sit beside him and try to make conversation, but second thoughts told him that was about the worst thing he could do. Ames was in no mood to be consoled by anyone, particularly Jeff.

When the bus came to a stop in the parking area of the YMCA camp, Jeff took his gym bag down off the rack and joined the others piling out the front exit. When he reached the door, he put his right foot out to step down, but at that instant somebody right behind him shouldered him roughly to one side and knocked him off-balance. With his right foot extended,

129

he was unable to regain his balance, and he pitched forward. He made a frantic grab with his free hand for the side of the door but missed it and went tumbling down.

The bus had stopped with the door just ahead of the front bumper of a parked car, and Jeff hit his head on the bumper as he fell. Fortunately, it was only a glancing blow, and he was just stunned for a second or two. Before others could reach out a hand to help, he was able to push himself up to his feet.

Then he saw Frank Ames striding toward the path leading to the tents, and he heard Ben Pinder's voice crack like a whip.

"Ames! Come back here!"

Frank stopped, turned, and came walking back slowly.

"Yeah?" he grunted.

"That was a pretty stupid thing to do, Ames," Pinder said evenly.

Ames raised his brows. "What was?" Then in a sneering tone, "Oh! You mean him falling on his face? Not my fault he tripped over his own feet."

"It was your fault, and you know it!" Pinder snapped. "I think you owe Jeff an apology."

Jeff opened his mouth to say something, but a swift look from Ben Pinder stopped the words from coming out.

"Well?" Pinder said, looking back to Ames. "What about it?"

Frank's face took on a stubborn look. "Why should I?" he said sullenly. "It wasn't my fault. He tripped."

Pinder shook his head. "No, he didn't," he said quietly. "I saw what happened. You knocked him off-balance when you shouldered him out of your way. So you owe Jeff an apology. Now!"

Ames's face twisted with anger, and he started to speak, but something in Pinder's steady look changed his mind. He licked his lips, swallowed, and looked at Jeff out of glowering eyes.

"Sorry," he muttered. He added quickly, "Only because he says so."

"Not good enough, Ames!" Pinder rapped out. "Try it again."

Frank Ames's face turned fiery red, and his black eyes glowed. He lifted the gym bag he carried and hurled it to the ground.

"I won't!" he raged at Pinder. "I've had it right up to here! I quit! I want out of this crummy setup."

"We'll talk about that later, Ames," Pinder said evenly. "Right now—"

"No!" Frank exploded. "I want out *now!* I'm sick of nursemaiding a bunch of little punks and being pushed around. I quit, and nobody's going to stop me!"

Pinder stared at him for a long moment, then nodded. "All right, Ames, have it your way," he said. "Go pack your gear and come up to the lodge. I'll pay you and arrange for your transportation back to Bedford."

Frank picked up the gym bag he'd hurled to the

ground and raked the group of counselors with eyes full of icy contempt.

"You stupid suckers!" he snarled. Turning on his heel, he strode along the path to the tents.

12 Promises Made

Two HOURS LATER Frank Ames was gone from the YMCA camp. For a day or so his blowup was a topic of general discussion, but soon after that he was forgotten. Ben Pinder put Bob Banks, a young member of his administrative staff, in charge of Ames's tent. It turned out that Banks was a basketball enthusiast and liked to play, so the counselors were not short one man when they got together for their daily practice game.

Camp life continued after that at an interesting and

enjoyable level, and three weeks before the end of the season, Ordway returned the YMCA camp's visit. Again the YMCA youngsters won their rough-and-tumble game. And again the Ordway counselors gave the YMCA counselors some very good experience but no chance at all to win.

Departure day for the eighty kids was almost as hectic as arrival day had been, but eventually the three buses rolled away with everybody safely aboard. Most of the administrative and counselor staffs stayed another two days to close up the camp. Then they said their good-byes and headed for their homes, Jeff and Paul driving back to Bedford in the Chevrolet.

School started one week later, and finally the day came that Jeff had waited for so long: the first day of basketball practice.

It was much the same as it had been the previous year. Some seventy-five hopefuls reported to Coach Doc Parks, and it was a week or so before he was able to get a look at all of them and sort them into small squads. The one big difference for Jeff was that this year he was not assailed by doubts and worries about making the cuts. He felt confident that, barring an unforeseen accident, he would make the team. Right at the start Jeff was one of the ten Doc Parks named to work out on the first two squads. Eight of the others had been counselors at the YMCA camp. The ninth was a husky redhead named Joe Hern, who had played a

year of varsity basketball at Belmont High and transferred this year to Bedford. The only YMCA counselor
not in the group was Jack Bevins, who had graduated
the previous year.

Another thing that was satisfying to Jeff was the
matter of Frank Ames. More than once after Ames
quit camp, Jeff had wondered how things were going to
be when the Bedford High basketball season started.
Ames obviously hated Jeff. It was silly to think
otherwise. So how would Ames act, and what would he
do? As team captain, Ames swung a certain amount of
weight. Would he use it in some sort of retaliation
against Jeff?

These questions, and a few others, seemed to be
answered in the first week or so of practice. Frank
Ames showed no sign, by word or deed, of animosity
toward Jeff. On the other hand, neither did he show any
indication that bygones were bygones and that friendship
was possible. If anything, Ames had become even more
of a loner than before—one who couldn't care less about
the rest of the world, just as long as he was left to
himself.

Yet there was something else about Frank Ames.
He seemed a little the way he had the first few days at
the YMCA camp. He didn't go around wearing that
superior smile too much, nor did he do a lot of talking.
It was something else. The best Jeff could guess was
that Ames was taking his duties as team captain very
seriously. It seemed almost as if Ames were trying to

set himself up as a model for all the others to pattern themselves after.

Whatever it was that Ames was trying to be suited Jeff fine. He certainly had no desire to engage in any kind of vendetta with Ames. If Frank chose not to be antagonistic toward him, that was all the better. At any rate, things progressed most favorably for Jeff. Each day of practice Jeff was able to make his plays a bit smoother. By the end of three weeks, Doc Parks had reduced the squad to twenty and apparently picked Ames, Jeff, Hal Allen, Dan Logan, and Joe Hern as his first-string five. Those five scrimmaged a part of each day's practice session against a team made up of the others and often remained after practice for a blackboard session with Parks.

By the time Parks made his final cut, he had them well drilled in both offense and defense and functioning like a well-oiled machine. In past years Doc Parks had always had great confidence in his teams—always sure they would go all the way. This year he was being a little more cautious. He still had confidence in Bedford's team, but he refrained from making predictions that Bedford would go all the way to the state championship.

The day before the final squad cut, the dormant friction between Jeff and Frank Ames suddenly came to the surface. Jeff was not surprised, because for the last few days he'd had the feeling that Ames was burning inside. Three or four times, when Jeff had made a spectacular basket right after Ames had failed to, the old familiar fire had glittered in Frank's eyes.

This time there was no question about it because the ill feeling simmering in Ames suddenly boiled to the surface. It happened during a fast-break drill designed to polish ball handling. Jeff was to pass to Ames and get the ball right back, both on the run. But when Ames took the pass, he was moving closer to Jeff. From a distance of less than ten feet, he snapped the ball back sharply. The spinning ball knocked Jeff's reaching hands apart and slammed into his face. The force of the ball knocked him back a step, and Jeff felt as if his nose had been flattened against his face.

It took a few seconds for his eyes to stop watering and his vision to clear, and by then the other players had gathered about him.

"You all right, Jeff?" Paul Young asked.

He took a breath and nodded. "Yeah, I'm okay," he said. "No damage."

As he spoke, he looked at Frank Ames and saw the hint of a smirk on his lips and the pleased gleam in his black eyes. Then the look vanished, and Ames quickly put out his hand.

"Gee, I'm—sorry," he grunted. "Okay?"

Jeff was so surprised that it was a split second before he could put out his own hand. As he did, though, he suddenly understood the reason for Ames's apology. Doc Parks had come over from the bench and pushed his way through the group.

"You hurt, Jeff?" the coach asked, peering at him. "You want to take a breather?"

"No," Jeff told him. "I'm okay."

A frown showed on the coach's brows. He glanced at Ames and back at Jeff. "Okay. Two more of you try it. And be careful."

Later the two teams resumed action in a scrimmage emphasizing the fast break. After a few ball exchanges, Jeff found himself paired with Frank on a two-on-one break, but this time Ames's pass to Jeff was one he was able to take with his hands and not his face. As practice continued, and Jeff's sore nose reminded him of what had happened, he got madder. When he thought of the quick switch in Ames's attitude when he'd obviously seen Doc Parks coming, Jeff got madder still. He was determined to retaliate, just as he had at the YMCA camp when Ames had started playing dirty basketball.

The opportunity presented itself about five minutes before the end of practice. It was during the execution of a play pattern that was almost the same as the one in which Jeff was hit. He was to take a pass from Ames and flip it right back. He put every bit as much smoke on the basketball as Ames had, but it did not push through Frank's hands and hit him in the face. Ames turned his face away, but the ball caught him square on the side of the head. He went down sideways to the floor. Jeff ran over quickly to bend down and help Ames to his feet.

"Hey, I am sorry, Frank!" he said, mock concern in

his voice. "I thought you'd be able to handle it. Are you all right, Frank?"

Ames didn't say anything. He pulled away from Jeff and leaned over to brace his hands on his knees and take a deep breath. When he straightened up a moment later, his eyes were glowing like hot coals again. He didn't speak, but only because he didn't get the chance. Doc Parks, who had trotted over, was doing the talking.

"Well, now that you two are even," he said quietly, looking from one to the other, "we'll call practice quits for today. Go shower and dress, everybody. Same time, same place, tomorrow."

With a nod, the coach pushed his way out of the group and headed for his office. The players headed for the locker rooms.

The swelling of his nose had gone down by the time Jeff woke up the next morning. There was no particular soreness, except when he pressed it with his fingers.

When he arrived at school that morning, there was a note from Parks in his homeroom, asking him to drop by the coach's office before practice that afternoon. Jeff speculated all morning, but was unable to reach any conclusion by the time he rapped lightly on Doc Parks's office door. He entered and was relieved when the coach smiled as he looked up from his desk.

"Sit down, Jeff," Parks said, nodding at the chair on the other side of the desk. "Be right with you."

He sat in the chair and it was a minute before Parks

pushed aside some papers he was working on and looked at him again.

"How's the nose?" the coach asked.

"Fine," Jeff assured him. "Couldn't be better."

"Good. Glad to hear it." Doc Parks picked up a pencil from the desk, leaned back in his chair, and rolled it slowly between his fingers. "Jeff, there're a couple of things I wanted to talk to you about," he said. "First, the way your playing has improved since last season. I want you to know I'm mighty pleased. I don't hand out unwarranted compliments. I consider you twice the player you were last year."

"Thank you, sir," Jeff said. "The credit belongs to Ben Pinder."

Doc Parks smiled. "Yes, I know about Ben," he said. "I don't know whether he told you, but he came to me to see if I had any objections to his taking you under his wing. I didn't, of course. No more than I objected to Ben hiring just about the entire Bedford basketball squad to be counselors at his YMCA camp. I don't know of any man better qualified to teach basketball than Ben Pinder."

"He's pretty terrific," Jeff said. "And I guess I can say that from experience."

Doc Parks chuckled. "Yes, I guess you can. He certainly did wonders with you. But *you* had to possess the natural ability and the drive to learn."

"You've helped me a lot, too, Coach," Jeff said in all sincerity.

141

Parks chuckled again. "Flattery will get you nowhere, young fellow," he said. "Fact is, in this case it's not even required. I imagine that you've surmised by now that you'll be playing at a guard spot this season. I'm expecting big things from you, Jeff. You'd better not let me down."

"I'll try not to, sir," Jeff said, "and that's a promise. I honestly think we've got a great team this year and that we'll go all the way."

The faint smile faded and Doc Parks's face sobered. He watched his fingers rolling the pencil for a moment, then took a deep breath. "That will depend on several things," he said quietly. "That's the other thing I wanted to talk to you about. You and Frank Ames."

Jeff could feel his face redden during the brief silence before Doc Parks continued.

"I know about what happened at the YMCA camp last summer," Doc Parks said, looking at him intently, "but that is none of my concern. I am also aware of the little byplay between you and Ames yesterday. That *is* my concern." The coach paused and leaned forward a little in his chair. "You know what I'm talking about, don't you?" he said.

"Yes, sir," Jeff replied, then added, before he could check the words, "but I didn't start it, Coach."

"I didn't say you did," Parks said quietly. "Whether you or Frank started it is not the important thing. What *is* important to me—very important—is that you're using Bedford's basketball court for your per-

142

sonal battleground. And *that* I will not permit!"

He paused for a moment to allow time for his words to sink in, and then continued. "I've kept my eye on you two ever since practice started," he said, "and I was pleased with what I saw. It looked as if you had put aside your feud and were giving basketball all your attention. But yesterday's business proved my thinking wrong. Your feud burst out into the open, and there's no indication that it won't happen again and again. That's why I have spoken to Frank, and that's why I'm speaking to you."

Once again the coach paused, this time to take a deep breath. "With you and Ames at the guard spots," he said, "Bedford should have a fine team; without you two, just mediocre. But I'd rather put a mediocre team on the court, with everybody fighting to win, than a fine team, with two of its star players fighting each other at the expense of the team. Believe me, I would!"

Jeff nodded slowly, and Coach Parks went on.

"Any player I coach gives one hundred percent effort on the court one hundred percent of the time, or he doesn't play for me. What you and Frank Ames do *off* the court is *your* business, but what you do *on* the court is *my* business. I've said this to Frank, and now I'll say it to you, Jeff. I am not demanding that you make up and become friends. All I am demanding is that, on the court, you forget your differences and concentrate on playing your best basketball. If you don't—if there is so much as a hint of what happened yesterday—you both will be dropped from the team. Now, in case I haven't made myself absolutely clear, are there any questions?"

"Only this, sir," Jeff said after a moment's thought. "What if it's one-sided? I mean, what if one of us starts something, but the other ignores him? Will we both still get dropped?"

"No," Parks told him. "Frank asked me that same question. I told him that I intend to be watching during practice as well as during a scheduled game. If I see anything like that, I'll drop the guilty one from the team. I don't expect that to happen, however. I don't believe Ames is a fool; neither are you. Both of you love basketball too much. Now, does that answer your question?"

Jeff nodded. "Yes, sir, that's fair enough for me. I won't give you that kind of trouble."

"Nor will Ames, I feel quite sure," Parks said. He smiled and stood up. "Well, that's all I had to say to you, Jeff. I just wanted to count on you two delivering, and now I feel sure you will. Better go get into your suit now. I'll be out in a few minutes."

"Yes, sir," Jeff said and went out into the gym.

As Jeff stepped out of the office, Frank Ames was passing by on his way to the dressing room. Ames stopped and looked at Jeff, then at Parks's office door, and back to Jeff again.

"That's right," Jeff said with a nod. "He just talked to me, too. You want to make a deal? Just play basketball? A time-out on grudges?"

Ames gave him a long hard stare and nodded.

"Deal," he grunted and pushed open the locker-room door.

13 Opening-Game Test

BEDFORD'S OPENING GAME of the season was against Natick High, a team they had beaten by only two points last year. Natick had not lost a single regular through graduation or transfer. Preseason analyses coupled Bedford and Natick as favorites to win the conference title. In view of the fact that they were facing each other in the season's opening game, it was generally believed that the title issue could be settled right then and there.

It was also believed, in the Bedford camp, that their chances of winning depended upon how well they could stop Jan Muntz, the Natick star. Muntz was a tow-headed, six-foot-six center who was as strong and as fast as a greyhound. He'd been Natick's outstanding star in his sophomore and junior years and had twice been named to the all-conference team. He was the subject of Coach Doc Parks's pregame talk to his players in the Bedford dressing room.

"I've said it all week, fellows, and I'll say it again," he told them. "Muntz is the key. Smother him and we can win. It's almost as easy as that. Your drills this week showed me you know how, so I'm not worrying. Keep your eyes open for new plays. They'll have a few for us —you can depend on that. But we'll cross that bridge when we come to it. Until then, the name of our game is *Muntz.* Any questions?"

Parks then named his starting five—Jeff and Ames at the guard spots and a front line of Hal Allen, Dan Logan, and Joe Hern. Minutes after that the coach led his squad out onto the court.

The opening game always did attract a large attendance, but for this game, so widely considered a crucial one for both teams, a record-breaking crowd had turned out. It was a complete sellout, plus an overflow. As the two squads warmed up at opposite ends of the court, the gym was a madhouse. The two school bands competed to drown out each other, and so did the two cheering sections. Not until the squads left the floor and

147

the referees took their positions did the uproar abate
to any degree. When the opposing lineups shook hands
and got set for the tap-off, a renewed swelling of
sound rose to the gym's rafters.

Jan Muntz's extra height and reach gave him a
clear edge over Dan Logan at the tap-off. Natick got
the ball, and they were off in high gear. They roared
upcourt in a series of short, quick passes and fed to
Muntz, who popped it in for first blood. The Natick
fans howled with glee, but before the echo had died
away, the Bedford team gave its fans something to yell
about. Jeff brought the ball out and flipped it to Ames,
who passed to Allen going down the left lane toward
the corner. Allen took it on the run, ducked away from
his man, and threaded a bounce pass to Logan at the
foul line. Dan feinted a jump shot, pulling Muntz off his
feet, and shoved an underhand pass to Jeff, who popped
it in as he cut under the basket.

Natick brought the ball out fast, but Bedford slowed
them down as they tried to work it in close and give
Jan Muntz a shot. Dan Logan was following Parks's
orders to the letter. He was all over the Natick star,
trying not to give him a moment's advantage. Muntz
suddenly took a quick feed, rolled for the basket in a
lightninglike movement, and scored again. Less than a
minute later, he hit from the corner to put Natick ahead
by four.

Stung by the two quick scores, Bedford stormed back
and scored on a bell ringer by Frank Ames. Then Dan

Logan outjumped Muntz at the Bedford board and shot a quick pass out to Jeff, breaking fast down the sidelines. Ames, also in motion, shot up the center, a half step ahead of his man, to take Jeff's pass and go the rest of the way for a lay-up. It was a nice bit of team play, and Doc Parks, sitting on the bench, smiled for the first time in the game.

That evened the score, and for the next three minutes the two teams chased each other up and down the court, with neither able to score. In the next minute, though, Natick won a rebound scramble under Bedford's basket and tipped it in, then added a third point when Hal Allen was whistled for hacking. Frank Ames immediately got two of the points back on a long jumper that brought a roar from the crowd. But the ball was barely back in play when Muntz outmaneuvered Dan Logan again and hit.

At the quarter, Natick was leading by four points. Parks sent in Pete Dixon for Logan, who was tiring fast. But Dixon was no match for the Natick star, and after two minutes and three goals, all by Muntz, Dan Logan went back into the game. He contained Muntz long enough for Bedford to rack up baskets by Jeff and Ames, but then the Natick star broke loose again for a score, followed quickly by a long one-hander by Jeff's opposing guard.

Parks gave Jeff and Ames a breather, sending in Paul and Dave Fasi to replace them. They played good ball, but it seemed that no sooner would Bedford start closing the gap than Natick would go on a scoring spree that opened up its lead even more. Led by Jan Muntz, their shooting was deadly, particularly at the foul line. It was mostly Muntz, though. His teammates were contributing something, but it was the tall tow-head who was almost single-handedly sinking Bedford. He simply was not being stopped and was only slowed down a little by Logan's efforts. Dan Logan was playing his heart out, but it was not nearly enough. Muntz was too strong and too fast. During the second quarter, Doc Parks made several substitutions and tried in various ways to reduce the Natick star's effectiveness, but none was successful.

If there was anything that Bedford could feel good about, it was that they were able to score pretty freely themselves and at least keep within striking distance. That, however, was not what won basketball games. It was no good to have an offense that could score points if the defense could not keep the other team from scoring more.

By the time the half ended, with Natick leading, 42–34, Doc Parks's face was grave and his brows were furrowed in deep thought. He didn't say anything as the team came off the court and headed for the dressing room. He didn't even look at them. He simply stood by the bench and did not move until the last Bedford player had passed him. Then he followed his squad into the dressing room. Closing the door behind him, he watched his tired players slump down on the benches and towel their sweaty faces.

"Relax, fellows," he said. "We've still got half a ball game left to play. We'll get those points back."

Dan Logan looked up from an orange he was sucking and wagged his head. "That Muntz!" he said with a groan. "He's not human!"

Parks nodded. "We haven't stopped him yet, but we will."

"How?" Logan asked wearily. "The only way to stop that guy is with a gun—I'm not even sure if that would do it."

"A gun's not the only way," Parks said with a faint smile. "There's another way, and I think it will do the trick." He paused, and when he had everybody's attention he continued. "They have one play that's worked for them almost every time," he said. "I didn't keep count, but I'd say that Muntz scored half his point total on it. In case you didn't notice, it goes like this: Cox, the guard, passes to Baker. Then Baker feeds the ball to Muntz, cutting off a simple pick from the other forward coming across, and the big guy rolls to the basket to score."

"Yeah!" Logan grunted. "Leaving me flapping my arms. He's a phantom, Coach! You see him now, and then he's gone."

"Don't feel too bad about it, Dan," Doc Parks soothed. "You've been doing a good job guarding Muntz, but it's a tough one for just one man. He requires double-teaming."

151

"But we have double-teamed him," Hal Allen spoke up. "He just passes off, and the man left unguarded hits for one."

"I know," Parks said. "Switching on Muntz can backfire on you, but I think we can do it on the one play I'm talking about and have the percentage with us. Now, here's what we'll do. When Cox passes to Baker he always heads for the corner, and Jeff goes right along with him. But Jeff won't do that anymore. He'll go only a few steps and then break over to the foul line and help Dan make Muntz change his mind about rolling for the basket. Get it?"

"But what about Cox?" Jeff wanted to know. "He's in the corner unguarded. Muntz only has to pass to Cox, and he'll have a wide-open shot at the basket."

Doc Parks nodded. "That's right. And that's what we *want* Cox to do—take the shot, because that will give us the percentage. We'll give Cox the corner shot. I've been watching him, and on five tries from the corner he hit only once. With Muntz shooting, it might be more like four out of five. That's a pretty good percentage in our favor, wouldn't you say?"

"I feel better already!" Dan Logan exclaimed with a grin. He pointed a finger at Jeff. "Keep your eyes open, pal."

"I'll be there," Jeff told him.

"Something else, Dan," Parks said to the tall center. "As soon as Muntz passes to Cox in the corner, you cut for the basket for the rebound. And you, Jeff—you'll

hang in to screen Muntz from the basket. All right, let's go through it again, so you all know just what to do. . . ."

The coach went over the play three more times. Then he had a few suggestions for individual players to better their performances in the second half. By the time he was through, it was time to go back out onto the court.

The Natick starting five came out on the floor obviously fired up to put Bedford down in the least possible time. They quickly took possession of the ball at the tap and swung into action.

They started right off on the play pattern that Doc Parks had discussed in the dressing room. Cox got the ball, passed to Baker, and then lit out for the left corner. Jeff stuck right with him for three full steps and then cut back over toward the key. By then Jan Muntz had taken the feed from Baker and was about to roll around Dan Logan and take his shot. With Jeff suddenly appearing out of nowhere, the big Natick star whipped the ball over to Cox in the corner. The guard took it, set himself, and shot.

The shot missed. The ball hit the rim and bounced straight up. Logan, a full step ahead of Muntz, went up for the ball and grabbed it. Logan came down with the rebound, took a step forward, and shot the ball out to the sidelines to start a fast break that caught the Natick defense napping and led to a quick score.

The sudden turn of events brought a roar of applause from the Bedford spectators, and as Jeff trotted back toward his end of the court, he saw the look of surprise on Jan Muntz's face. The surprise defensive play by Bedford, however, did not take any of the fire out of the Natick players. They brought the ball out fast and started to work upcourt once more, but a bad pass by Baker glanced off the tips of Muntz's fingers and went out-of-bounds. Frank Ames threw in for Bedford, a hard bouncing pass that Jeff took on the dead run, spinning on a dime to flip to Logan in the pivot. Dan feinted a shot at the basket and poked the ball under Muntz's outstretched arm to Ames. Frank drove hard and went up high to drop the ball in for another score. Less than a minute after that, Joe Hern hit from the corner, and Bedford was within two points of tying it up.

The Natick coach called time to huddle with his team and make a couple of substitutions.

When play was resumed, Natick scored in a matter of seconds, but Bedford got the two points right back when Hal Allen took a long pass from Ames and outran his man to lay it up. When Natick brought the ball out, they tried the same play pattern they had tried at the start of the half, and Bedford stopped it cold again. Natick tried that play twice more, and both times Bedford stopped it.

With their surefire scoring play stopped cold, Natick was not the basketball team it had been in the first half. They still played hard and fast, and Bedford had to battle for every point they scored against them. But the partial throttling of Muntz slowly took its toll. Bedford tied the score in the middle of the third period and then moved farther and farther out in front. Jeff and Dan Logan put on a show of brilliant ball handling and some accurate shooting.

Natick rallied to start off the fourth quarter with three quick baskets. For a couple of minutes it looked as if they were going to smother Doc Parks's boys, but the Bedford team managed to choke off the rally and start hitting. Frank Ames, who had been playing a fine game all along, suddenly caught fire. His floor work was fantastic, and he made scoring shots that had to be seen to be believed. That broke Natick's back. They continued to battle right down to the sounding of the horn, but it was a hopeless cause. Bedford walked off the floor the winner, 78–64. In the dressing room Doc Parks beamed at his players.

"Fine game," he said to them. "A mighty fine game. I'm proud of you."

"Thanks, Coach," Dan Logan said with a laugh. "But, if you ask me, *you* won this one for us."

The tall center's comment was instantly and loudly echoed by every other member of the squad.

14   "Beat Bedford!"

WINNING THE SEASON OPENER against Natick was a terrific boost for the Bedford players. Before the game,
they believed they had a topflight squad, and winning
proved them right. It did something else, too—it gave
them that added touch of confidence so essential in any
type of sport. Now they had confidence in themselves
individually, confidence in their teammates, and, of
course, confidence in their coach.

That was a combination hard to beat, and they proved

157

that to be a fact again and again. They won their next three games with no serious trouble, and after the Christmas and New Year's vacation, they picked up right where they had left off.

For Doc Parks it was something that every coach dreams about but seldom sees become a reality: a seemingly unbeatable first team, and, on the bench, second-stringers who were almost as good. In fact, the Bedford bench was so good that Parks could send in his first team to build up a comfortable lead in the opening quarter, then send in his second team to play most of the two middle quarters, and return his regulars to the floor in the fourth quarter to wrap it up. As a result, the bench got in almost as much playing time as the first team. As each player gained more and more experience on the court, the entire squad became more and more formidable. Doc Parks was not only building a winning team this year, but he was also laying the groundwork for a winning team next year.

With each conference win, Bedford increasingly became the center of attention in newspaper sports pages throughout the state. The pressure wasn't off for a minute. As their fame increased, so did the number of "Beat Bedford" posters in the stands at away-from-home games. Each win made Bedford more of a prize for any school that *could* beat them, and every game was a fight to the finish.

Jeff was doing exceptionally well. He enjoyed every minute of it. He was getting a lot of favorable comment in the sports pages of the newspapers—almost as much as Frank Ames, who was playing near-perfect basket-ball.

What pleased Jeff most was that Ames had not once come even close to breaking the truce between them. Frank Ames, of course, was still Frank Ames—the one hundred percent loner who much preferred to go his solitary way and was openly wary and suspicious of any-one who tried to get close to him. Since the truce they'd agreed upon outside Doc Parks's office door, Ames had in no way shown that he felt differently toward Jeff. Ames still looked at him out of eyes cold with dislike and still spoke to him only when it was absolutely neces-sary. But Ames refrained completely from committing any physical act on the basketball court to express his animosity. He cooperated with Jeff as a companion guard to the fullest extent. To Jeff, this meant he was able to give everything he had and not have to keep an eye out for any hostile move by Frank Ames. Jeff did not know what Doc Parks had said to Ames, but whatever it was, it had certainly done the trick.

As Bedford continued to win, both at home and away, Coach Doc Parks had but one major worry. His players could get so used to winning that they'd become overconfident and unconsciously let down. Fully realiz-ing that this could easily happen, he took every measure he could to prevent it. But it did happen in the next to the last game on the schedule, and so did a couple of other things—the kind that give coaches gray hair.

The game was with Weston High School and was expected to be another win for Bedford. Weston had lost six of its games, and one sportswriter stated in his column that the best play Weston could make would be not to show up. That particular story was the talk of the town after the Weston game.

Weston had really nothing to lose but a great deal to gain. To knock off the first-place team would be quite a feather in their cap and would make up for such a poor season record. And they could play loose, under no strain or tension about their reputation if they lost.

On the other hand, it was exactly the opposite for Doc Parks's men. Although they had won fourteen straight games, the strain and the tension were the same in every game. Now they were within only two games of capturing the conference title. As good as they were, they could not risk taking any chances, and they knew it.

As usual, Doc Parks sent in Ames, Jeff, Allen, Logan, and Hern as his starting team. Bedford grabbed the tap, then quickly worked the ball upcourt for the first score of the game. Weston brought the ball out, but they had hardly crossed the center line when Jeff darted away from his man to knock down a pass and race after the loose ball. He scooped it up and drove hard for a lay-up. The ball did not drop through. It hit the rim and bounced off.

Jeff was so sure he would score that he had turned from under the basket and was two steps away when the ball bounced off the hoop. He slammed on the brakes and spun around but was too late to retrieve the ball. A Weston player raced by him to take the ball on the dead run and dribble it a few steps before passing the length of the court to a teammate who had broken into the clear. He dropped it in for a score, with no Bedford player within ten feet of him.

"Forget it," Dan Logan said as Jeff trotted by him to bring the ball in. "It can happen to anybody."

"Yeah, but it happened to *me*," Jeff muttered under his breath as he took the ball from the referee at the baseline.

Jeff brought the ball out and passed to Ames, who whipped the ball to Hal Allen. Allen feinted a long shot and passed over to Jeff, who had broken away from his man, and Jeff fed a bounce pass to Logan in the pivot. Logan had a clean shot at the basket and missed. Frank Ames raced in to grab the rebound and push it in, but the ball hit the rim and bounced free. Logan got hold of it again and hooked one up as he fell away from the basket. The ball hit the edge of the backboard and ricocheted out-of-bounds. Doc Parks signaled for time and walked to the edge of the court to meet his team.

"You fellows trying to make it easy for them or hard for yourselves?" he asked.

"Sorry, Coach," Dan Logan said. "I guess I was pretty lousy."

"Likewise," Jeff said. "That lay-up should have gone in."

Frank Ames didn't say anything, but the look on his

161

face clearly indicated he wasn't pleased with his own playing.

Doc Parks grinned faintly. "All right, let's get back in there and play some basketball!"

The players nodded, pressed hands for luck, and moved back onto the floor. Weston put the ball back in play from their baseline. They worked it past mid-court and drove down toward the top of the key with a series of quick passes. There a pass to a corner man was slapped down by Joe Hern. Dan Logan grabbed the ball on the first bounce and flipped it across his body to Frank Ames, breaking into the clear up the middle. Ames drove hard for the basket and went up high to pop it in, but he missed the shot again. The ball hit the rim, hung suspended for a moment, and fell off to the left into the hands of a Weston player, who started a fast break with a midair flip to the sidelines. Before Bedford could get back on defense, Weston had another two points.

Doc Parks jumped up off the bench as though he were going to call another time-out, but he didn't. He glared out at the floor, whacked his clipboard against the palm of his hand, and sat down again. It was lucky for Bedford that he didn't call for time, because a moment later they came charging upcourt and scored on a nice corner shot by Joe Hern. Then Hal Allen stole the ball and hit for another quick two points.

Bedford gained possession again on a turnover, and Dan Logan scored with a short jumper. It began to

look as if the Bedford team had snapped out of its trance and was ready to play basketball. Twenty seconds later a Weston player grabbed a bad pass by Frank Ames and went streaking to the basket for a score. Then Jeff pulled a boner that brought a burst of laughter from the Weston fans.

In a situation that was tailor-made for it, Jeff tried the behind-the-back dribble, to elude his guard, who was harrying him in the backcourt. He completely missed the ball with his left hand, and a Weston defender grabbed it and was off and flying for a lay-up. The burst of laughter from the Weston seats set his cheeks on fire.

A minute or so later, when Dan Logan missed a shot he normally could have made with his eyes closed, that was enough for Doc Parks. He pulled out Jeff, Ames, and Logan, and sent in Paul, Dixon, and Hall. The substitutions resulted in a Bedford basket, but Weston got it back just as the quarter ended, and that gave them a one-point lead.

The same Bedford lineup took the floor for the second quarter and held its own against the fired-up Weston team. After a minute or so of chasing each other up and down the court, Weston suddenly hit for two. Bedford came right back to rack up two for themselves, but shortly after, Weston was awarded a free shot when one of its players was fouled in the act of shooting by Dixon. The foul try was good, completing a three-point play, and Bedford got possession of the ball.

They didn't do much with it, and when Weston got

the ball back and scored twice in quick succession, Doc Parks sent Jeff, Ames, and Logan back into the game. They got right down to business and played serious basketball, but they still couldn't seem to hit with any regularity. They peppered the Weston basket with shots, but nothing seemed to drop through the hoop.

When the half ended, Bedford trailed by six big points. Another hot streak by Weston could blow the game wide open.

In the locker room between halves Doc Parks didn't say much to his squad. There really wasn't very much he could say. They were not making mistakes in the execution of their various play patterns; it was their shooting accuracy that was way off. When one usually effective scorer has a bad game, it's something to be expected, because it happens to the best of players. But when the three best scorers on a team have a bad game all at the same time. . . .

Doc Parks simply made one or two minor suggestions, spoke a few words of encouragement, and mentally crossed his fingers. He sent the first team back in to start the third quarter and hoped for the best.

The half-time rest caused little change in his star trio. Their shooting accuracy was not improved to any degree. Halfway through the third quarter Jeff suddenly got hot and scored three quick baskets, but then he promptly cooled off and missed his next five tries by wide margins.

Sensing the good possibility of pulling off a big upset,

Weston was playing way over their heads. The Weston fans went wild with joy, and the Bedford fans watched in silent disbelief. It just couldn't be happening. But it was. The best team in the league was taking it on the chin from the worst team in the league. Bedford was scoring now and then and managing to hang in close, but that was all. They missed the shots that would have tied it up and put them out in front. In a frantic effort to ignite some kind of spark, Doc Parks substituted repeatedly but failed to alter the score in Bedford's favor. The game went into the final quarter with Weston out in front by six points.

The fourth quarter was one that was to be talked about for some time afterward—especially the last four minutes of it. Doc Parks's prayers, and those of hundreds of Bedford fans in the seats, were answered. As if by magic, Jeff, Ames, and Dan Logan recovered their shooting eyes and ran wild against Weston. They sank shot after shot and swept the Weston players right off the court. When there were two minutes to go, they had evened it up. And when the horn finally sounded, Bedford had won, 68–62.

As the team headed for the locker rooms, there was no show of jubilation. They were a quiet bunch; they had been given a scare and were still shaking a little. In the locker room, Doc Parks summed it up for everybody.

"That's the sloppiest win I've ever seen," he said solemnly.

Five days later Bedford romped over Arlington High School, 74–59, to win the conference title. Two weeks after that they had clinched their Class A state tournament berth with the last in a series of lopsided victories.

15 *A Personal Matter*

THE FOUR CLASS A high schools competing for the state basketball championship were Bedford, Malden, Troy, and Concord. The tournament would be held Friday and Saturday evenings of the week following the end of the regular season, at the Bedford Arena. The pairings for Friday night pitted Bedford against Troy, and Malden against Concord. The two winning teams on Friday night would meet for the championship on Saturday night, with the two losing teams playing for consolation honors. The collective opinion of the sports-writers placed Malden as the pretournament favorite, with Bedford a dark horse.

Perhaps Coach Doc Parks was a little upset by having his team rated the tournament underdog, because the practice sessions during the regular season were mere child's play compared to the practice sessions during the week before the tournament. Never an easy taskmaster, Parks drilled his team for long hours every day. He made it plain to one and all that he would not be satisfied with anything less than perfection. The players, no doubt a little burned themselves at not being rated the tournament favorites, responded with one hundred percent effort.

At the end of the last practice session, Dan Logan expressed the sentiment of the entire squad: "If we're not ready for them now, we never will be!"

The first game of the Friday night doubleheader was between Malden and Concord. It was scheduled to start at seven thirty, and by seven o'clock the oval-shaped Bedford Arena was solidly packed from floor to rafters. The whole place was a blaze of color and jumping with sound. Jeff sat with the other members of the Bedford squad in the bottom row of seats, close to a ramp that led down to the dressing rooms. At half time of the first game, they would go down to the dressing rooms and get ready for their game. Doc Parks had arranged it so they could watch the play until then.

"I want you fellows to get a good look at the team

169

you're going to beat for the championship," he said to them. "So keep your eyes open, and remember what you see. It might come in handy Saturday night."

The Malden and Concord squads completed their warm-up, the opening ceremonies were conducted, and the two starting fives moved back onto the floor. There was a momentary hush and then a mounting roar of sound as the ball was tossed up for the tap. Malden gained possession of the ball and immediately went to work and scored. Concord charged right back to do the same thing, and then it was Malden's turn again.

For the first three or four minutes it was a two-sided affair, but then the Malden squad started to show why they had been named the tournament favorites. They had an overall advantage in height and weight, and they were a hard-running, fast-breaking team that applied the pressure without a moment's letup. Most important was the fact that every man on the squad was a deadly shot from the floor as well as from the foul line.

If they had one outstanding player, it was Pete Collins. He was a smoothly muscled guard who could fly like the wind, turn on a dime, and hit from any angle, either far out or close in to the basket. Jeff watched him attentively, because if Bedford did meet Malden for the championship, Pete Collins would be his defensive assignment.

Concord played well and fought tenaciously. They just didn't possess that extra something that would enable them to take charge of the action. When the half ended, and Jeff and his teammates headed for the dressing rooms, Malden was leading, 39–33.

When the Bedford and Troy teams came up from the dressing rooms, Malden had beaten Concord, 78–68, and had won the right to play in the state championship game. As the Bedford team started warming up, the Malden fans were still cheering about their victory. The Troy squad was warming up at the other end of the court, and what the Bedford squad saw did not give them any assurance of an easy victory. The Troy players were big, and they seemed well able to move and shoot. It appeared that Bedford had work cut out for it.

It was something of a surprise when, once play was started, it became apparent that Troy was completely outclassed, on this occasion, at least. In the opening quarter, Bedford's first team ran them ragged, piling up twenty points to Troy's nine. In the second quarter, Bedford's first team rode the bench while the second team saw some action and extended the lead to sixteen points.

The second half was not much different. Parks played his first-stringers no more than one or two at a time, and only so they could get in some extra practice for Saturday's game. Apparently Troy had reached its peak in winning its conference title, and instead of being able to hold the keen edge, they had instead incxplicably lost their sharpness. It was almost an act of mercy when the game-ending horn sounded, with

Bedford coming out on top, 86–59.

As soon as he was dressed, Jeff went out of the Arena and over to his aunt's car in the parking lot. His aunt Kate and Ben Pinder were waiting for him in the car.

"Congratulations!" his aunt said.

Jeff grinned and gave a little twist of his head. "Thanks, but who deserves it?" he said. "I feel sorry for those poor guys. They were way off their game tonight. Right now they must be wanting to shoot themselves."

"I imagine so," Ben Pinder said. "I can remember a couple of times toying with the same thought after we'd been blasted off the floor. It really hurts deep when you have a game like that. But that's the way it can be sometimes."

"The rough part is that Troy is really a good team," Jeff said. "Their season's record proves it."

"That's basketball," Pinder said with a shrug. "Sometimes records don't mean a thing."

"No, I guess not," Jeff agreed. He suddenly smiled. "But if Malden pulls the same thing Saturday night, I won't be sorry at all!"

"Don't count on it," Pinder said flatly. "That team won't lose its edge."

"I'm not counting on a thing," Jeff assured him, "except a real rough battle."

"May I make a suggestion?" Kate Martin spoke up. "How about going out for a hamburger somewhere nearby?"

Pinder smiled at her. "You took the words right out of my mouth," he said. "Let's go."

They got into the car and, with Pinder at the wheel, drove to a popular little restaurant nearby.

When they were seated and had ordered, Jeff spoke up. "What do you think about Saturday's game, Ben? You saw Malden tonight, and you've seen us lots of times. Who's your choice?"

Pinder chuckled and shook his head. "Oh, no, you're not putting me on the spot," he said. "I'm not about to be hanged for treason."

"You mean you really think Malden will win, Ben?" Kate Martin asked quickly.

"No, I don't mean that," he said, shaking his head again. "Sentimentally, of course, I'm all for Bedford. But from a practical standpoint I—well, I just don't know. I really can't make a choice."

"A toss-up, huh?" Jeff grunted.

"Yes, a toss-up," Pinder admitted. "Bedford has a fine team. I'd even call it a great team. But from what I saw tonight, so has Malden. But that's only one game, and it may have been the best game they've played all season. It could be a mistake to evaluate Malden on just tonight's showing. Let's leave it at that, shall we? A toss-up—but our hopes all for Bedford. Okay?"

"Okay," Jeff said as his aunt nodded. "But tell me this: What do you think of that guard of theirs—Collins?"

"He's good," Pinder replied quickly. "He's going to

give you a very busy evening."

"Yes, I've figured that," Jeff said with a grimace. "Collins is plenty good."

"There's one thing I noticed, though," Pinder said. "Perhaps you did, too. He's not half as good moving to his left as he is to his right."

"No, I didn't spot that," Jeff admitted. "To me he was blue lightning either way."

"Oh, he's fast either way," Pinder said, "but faster to the right than to the left. You talk it over with Doc Parks and see what he thinks, but if I were playing Collins, I think I'd play him a bit loose to his left and tight to his right. There's a possibility that might discourage him from going right so often. If it does, then his effectiveness will be reduced at least a little. And, as the man said, every little bit helps."

"Hey, I'll do that!" Jeff said. "Talk it over with Doc Parks, I mean. Maybe he spotted that, too."

"My guess is that he did," Pinder said. "There's very little that happens on a basketball court that escapes his eyes." Pinder suddenly stopped and looked at his wristwatch. "Almost forgot to tell you two," he spoke again. "I'm flying to Denver late tonight."

"Denver?" Jeff echoed. "What's in Denver?"

"A little business meeting I've got tomorrow morning," Pinder replied.

"YMCA stuff?" Jeff probed. Then suddenly he gasped, "Hey, you're not being *transferred* to Denver, are you?"

174

Ben Pinder shook his head. "No, this trip has nothing to do with the Y," he said. "It's a personal matter."

Jeff glanced at his aunt for some clue.

"Don't look at me," she said. "I'm as much in the dark about this as you are."

Then the thought struck Jeff. "Ben—you'll miss the championship game tomorrow night! After all the—"

"Whoa! Not so fast!" Ben scowled at Jeff. "I'm certainly not going to miss *that* game. I'll be flying back tomorrow afternoon."

"We'll meet you at the airport, have dinner at home, and then drive to the arena," Kate Martin said.

"Thanks. That'll be great." Ben looked at Jeff, who hadn't eaten much, and grinned. "Something bothering you, friend?"

Jeff looked up. "Who, me?" he grunted. "Not a thing."

"Good," Pinder said, still grinning. "I thought you might be upset about my Denver trip."

Jeff peered at him, eyes narrowed slightly. "Why should I be?"

Pinder chuckled. "Good question," he said. "The truth is, you have a perfect right to wonder about it, because you're one reason I'm taking the trip."

"Me?" Jeff looked up.

"You're one reason," Pinder said. "Your aunt's another reason. But that's all I'm going to tell you now. I have a deal just about wrapped up in Denver. I'll tell you all about it when I get back in the afternoon."

Jeff stared at him in exasperation and then looked

175

at his aunt with an inquiring glance.

"Maybe," she suggested, "if you twist one of his arms, and I twist the other one—"

Pinder laughed. "Go ahead. But you'll find that I'm the strong, silent type. I won't break under torture."

"I suppose we'll just have to wait till tomorrow, then," Kate sighed.

"Don't lose any sleep over it," Pinder said casually.

Jeff moaned. "Oh, I'm really going to sleep *well* tonight. Not only the championship game tomorrow, but now this—this secret. I may as well not even go to bed tonight!"

All three laughed and rose to leave the restaurant.

"Not even a hint?" Jeff asked as they got into the car.

"I've said enough already," Pinder answered and slapped Jeff's back. "You'll know soon enough—tomorrow before the big game."

16 Trouble Comes in Twos

BEN PINDER was taking Union Airlines Flight 283 and would arrive at the Bedford Airport at four thirty Saturday afternoon. On Saturday morning Jeff attended a light workout and blackboard session in the gym, and shortly before four o'clock he and his aunt drove to the airport.

"Well, it won't be long now," Jeff said as he turned the car off the freeway onto the airport road. "And thank goodness for that! Boy, has it been a sweat!"

"So I've noticed," his aunt said with a laugh. "You've done more talking about Ben's trip than about the game tonight."

"And you haven't been curious at all, huh?" Jeff said. *"Sure* you haven't!"

"Of course I've been curious," Kate Martin told him, "but I saw no reason to get in a stew over it."

Jeff took his eyes off the road long enough to give her a glance. "He really didn't say anything to you?" he questioned. "Not even a hint?"

"Not even a hint," his aunt said firmly. "And to answer your next question—no, I didn't ask him anything, either!"

"Okay, okay, but it sure floors me," Jeff said with a frown. "Why would *I* be a reason for his going to Denver?"

"Why would *I* be a reason?" his aunt countered.

Jeff took a deep breath and blew it out. "We'll soon know, huh?" he said.

He parked the car in the airport lot, and they went up the escalator to the lobby level of the terminal and to the Union Airlines counter, where they could check the arrival and departure board. There was a large crowd already around the counter, and it was a moment before Jeff and his aunt could get close enough to see the board. When they took a look at it, though, there was no arrival time or gate number posted for Flight 283. Instead the words NOT KNOWN YET were chalked on the board.

"What's that 'Not Known Yet' for Flight Two-Eight-Three mean?" Jeff asked one of the two ticket agents behind the counter.

There was a harassed look on the agent's face. He kept his voice under control as he replied. "Contact with the aircraft has been lost," he said. "Thirty minutes before it was to land at St. Louis. No word since. They had to go through a big storm front just out of Denver. As soon as we get word, we'll post it on the board."

"You mean it's *crashed?*" Jeff gasped before he could check the words.

The agent gave him a reproving look. "No, I don't mean that," he said. "All we know for sure is that Flight Two-Eight-Three is unreported at St. Louis and radio contact is lost. Why don't you go sit down and wait? We'll post any word the minute we get it."

Jeff and his aunt pushed their way out of the crowd in front of the counter and went over to one of the lobby benches to sit down. A queasy feeling had settled in the pit of Jeff's stomach, and he licked his lips nervously.

"Gee, I don't like this," he said, only half conscious that he was speaking aloud.

"I don't like it myself," his aunt said in a small voice.

He looked at her and saw the paleness of her face. "Everything's probably okay," he said, hoping to allay her fears. "A plane's radio going out is nothing new. Happens often. I bet when we find out, it'll be that they got lost in the storm for a little while and decided to pass up St. Louis and come straight on here. And we'll find

179

out soon, too. It will be just a matter of minutes."

"I hope so," his aunt said and smiled wanly.

For a few minutes they sat silent, glancing often at the flight board. Fifty or more people had now gathered in front of it, but each time they looked the words were the same. Jeff happened to notice a row of soft drink and snack machines at the far end of the lobby and turned to his aunt.

"Want a Coke or something?" he asked, pointing.

"No, thanks," she said. "I don't feel like anything."

Neither did he, and they lapsed into silence again. The minute hand of the lobby clock moved slowly around the face of the dial. Four times in the next hour Jeff went over to the Union Airline counter, but the answer to his question was always the same: "No word yet." Each time, the queasy sensation in the pit of his stomach intensified.

At the end of an hour and a half of waiting, Kate Martin drew in a deep breath and got to her feet. "Well, we'd better go home," she said, with just the faintest tremor in her voice. "I'll get you something to eat and you can take the car to the game. I'll stay at home in case Ben tries to reach us. And I can keep checking with Union Airlines, too, in case any word does come through."

Mention of the game came as a shock to Jeff. In his anxiety over the unreported airplane, he had completely forgotten about the championship game.

"Forget the game," he said impulsively. "I'll stay

FLIGHT	FROM	ARRIVALS	TIME
283	DENVEP		NOT KNOWN YET
116	ALABIDA		6:45
145	NO GAGE		7:27
26	CULEMBIX		8:10
206			

with you, Aunt Kate, and—"

"You'll do nothing of the sort!" she said sharply. "Sitting home with me won't change anything. Besides, it would be downright silly. You've got an important game to play. For you *and* for every other member of the team, not to mention Ben. You can't let them down, and you're not going to."

Jeff drew in a deep breath and let it out slowly, nodding. "You're right," he murmured. He took one more look at the flight board, but there had been no change. "Okay, let's go," he said.

They drove home, saying very little to each other and nothing about what may or may not have happened to Ben Pinder. Each thought of it constantly but did not speak for fear of further upsetting the other. When they reached the house, Jeff went immediately to the phone and called Union Airlines, but there was still no word, and no one knew when there would be.

At intervals of fifteen minutes after that, either he or his aunt called the airport, but it was the same thing each time. When they turned on the TV news, it only deepened their gloom and increased their fears. Violent thunder storms in the central states area had caused property damage, forced the cancellation of commercial airline flights, and even closed some airports. Flight 283 of Union Airlines was still unreported. Its fuel supply would have been exhausted a half hour before the news broadcast time. As soon as weather conditions permitted, the broadcast said, an extensive air search for the missing aircraft would be started.

Jeff had planned to sit with the Bedford team and watch the first half of the consolation game between Concord and Troy, but the unreported Flight 283 changed that. Hoping that the next phone call to the airport would result in some good news, he didn't leave the house for the Bedford Arena until the last minute.

During the short drive to the arena, he forced himself to focus all his thinking on the big game, and it took considerable effort. In a way, it was like waiting to learn the fate of a close member of the family. And the longer the waiting, the greater the worry and the anxiety.

Jeff parked his aunt's car in the lot behind the arena, took out his gym bag, and walked to the rear entrance. An attendant at the door looked at his competitor's card, then waved him on through. He entered the building and went down the flight of stairs leading to the locker rooms.

From the floor above came the faint sound of the high-school bands entertaining the spectators during half time, and he vaguely wondered what the Concord-Troy score was. He walked along the corridor until he came to a door with a card lettered BEDFORD tacked to it. He opened the door and stepped inside; instantly he knew that something was wrong. Instead of the excited chattering sounds of his teammates dressing for the game, there was only silence.

He saw Paul and the others seated in front of their

183

lockers in various stages of undress, but not one of them was speaking a word. Those who were moving were doing so in slow motion, and the others were simply sitting there, staring vacant-eyed at their locker doors. A strange, stifling feeling spread through Jeff's chest, and he hurried over to his locker, next to Paul's, and dropped his gym bag on the floor. Paul, who was staring down at his feet, looked up at him and nodded.

"Hi," he said listlessly. "Where've you been?"

"I got held up," Jeff said, brushing the question aside. "What's going on? Why's everybody so quiet?"

"We're sunk," Paul said heavily. "Frank Ames tripped on a bench and sprained his ankle. *He can't play.*"

Jeff felt as if he had been kicked in the stomach by a mule. It was a moment or two before he could speak. "Can't play?" he groaned. "Oh, no! You've got to be kidding!"

Paul jerked his head toward the far end of the row of benches. "Go see for yourself," he said.

Jeff looked in that direction and saw Ames sitting on the far end of the last bench, with Doc Parks on his knees in front of him, wrapping a large bandage around his right foot and ankle. Jeff approached them as Doc Parks got to his feet. The coach saw him and started to speak but gave him a tight-lipped look instead as he touched Ames on the shoulder.

"Sit tight, Frank," he said. "I'll get some crutches for you."

184

With that, Parks turned and walked rapidly along the row of lockers. Ames turned his head to look after him and saw Jeff. His eyebrows went up in mild surprise. "Finally showed up, eh?" Ames grunted. "We were beginning to wonder." As Frank spoke he gave a little laugh and pointed at his bandaged foot and ankle. "How about that, huh?"

"Gosh, Frank, I'm really sorry," Jeff said, sitting down on the bench beside Frank. "What a lousy thing to have happen. For the whole team. We need you to win."

Ames's eyes widened in even greater surprise. For a moment a look of warmth masked the glint of hardness in their depths. He gave another little laugh and batted the air with one hand. "Forget it," he said. "You guys will do all right without me. No big thing for me, anyway. I'm happy."

Jeff started incredulously. *"Happy?"* he exploded. "Happy because you can't play? What—"

"Of course not!" Ames's voice and eyes stopped him. "What kind of talk is that? Sure, I'd like to play, but I can't. So I should go cut my throat? I've finally got it made, see?"

Jeff gave a little shake of his head, as if to clear the cobwebs away. "What are you talking about?" he asked. "Got what made?"

Frank Ames chuckled, obviously enjoying Jeff's confusion. "The jackpot," he said. "Know what I got in the mail this morning? Basketball scholarship offers from *three* colleges. I may even get more before school's

185

out. So why shouldn't I be happy? You better believe it; I've really been sweating this college business. But no more. I'm *in!*"

A touch of envy, even jealousy, cut through Jeff, but it was gone in a flash. He reached out a hand and slapped Ames on the back. "Hey, that's wonderful, Frank!" he said, meaning it sincerely. "It's really great. Congratulations!"

A look of puzzled disbelief came into Ames's eyes. He stared at Jeff a moment and gave a little shake of his head. "A crazy world," he said tonelessly. "Real crazy!"

Jeff laughed. "What's crazy about it?" he asked.

Ames shook his head again. "Guess *I'm* crazy," he muttered. "Or was." A slow smile pulled back the corners of his mouth. "Funny thing," he murmured. "Last summer I got to hating you. You really had me scared. And I thought this scholarship bit would really cut you down, but it didn't. You tell me you're glad. Crazy."

"Sure, I'm glad, and there's nothing crazy about that," Jeff said. Then he added quickly, "Tell me this—what do you mean, I had you scared? I don't get it."

Frank Ames frowned and ran his fingers through his black hair. "Well, like this," he said slowly. "I've always wanted to go to college. But—well, with my setup, it was out, unless I could make it by the basketball scholarship route. So I latched on to that idea. My first

186

year playing for Bedford I did okay. Last year I really got the publicity. I was sure I'd catch the eyes of at least one college this year. Then you came along. Get it now?"

"No, I don't," Jeff told him. "What did I have to do with your plans?"

Ames peered at him hard, as if questioning Jeff's sincerity. He suddenly grinned ruefully. "Plenty," he said. "When somebody told me about your working out at the Y, I didn't think anything of it. But when I saw you playing at the Y camp, it hit me hard. You were *good!* Really good, and you'd be even better when the basketball season started. That's when I got scared. That's when I started really hating you."

"Scared of what?" Jeff asked. "Just because I'd improved? I still wasn't in your class; you must have seen that. What was there to be scared about?"

"I was scared you'd steal my stuff this season," Ames said after a moment's hesitation. "Get the big publicity instead of me. Maybe kill my chances for a scholarship. Now do you see what I mean?"

Jeff nodded. "Yes, I guess I do. But—who got the basketball scholarship offers, and who didn't? Doesn't that prove something?"

"Guess it does," Ames said with a contrite grin. He suddenly frowned and again ran his fingers through his hair. "About the Y camp thing," he said in a rush of words. "I'm really sorry about that. Okay?"

"Okay. Sure," Jeff said.

187

He was about to say more, but Doc Parks returned carrying a pair of crutches. The coach handed them to Ames and looked at Jeff.

"You'd better go get ready," he said quietly.

"Yes, sir," Jeff said and walked back to his locker.

17 Basket Fever

KEEP ON THE ALERT for their fast break," Doc Parks was saying, "and stick close to your man and keep up the pressure. When you see an opening to shoot, don't hesitate—shoot. The starting five will be Bates, Young, Allen, Logan, and Hern."

The Bedford coach paused for a moment and looked around at the silent, solemn-faced group around him.

"One more thing before you go out there," he continued. "Frank's accident is a bad break for us. But it only makes a tough job a little tougher, and that's all. Even without Frank, you're better than Malden, and I know you're going to prove it out there tonight. Hear that? I know you are going to win. And I know that you know it, too, in spite of what happened to Frank. I guess that's about it. Any last questions?"

There were none.

Doc Parks smiled and nodded. "All right," he said. "Let's go get 'em!"

If Doc Parks's words had succeeded in raising his players' spirits any, it was not reflected in their faces as they followed him out of the dressing room and up the ramp to the main floor. Their appearance brought a roar from the Bedford section. Excitement pulsed through the stands, almost like a fever—a basket fever. It continued as they went out onto the court for their warm-up. The Malden squad was already busy at the other basket, and as Jeff looked their way, he got the wild impression that they had all grown six inches taller since last night. They were a team of giants; there was no other word for them. The fluid ease with which they moved in and out under the basket added a few more butterflies to those already fluttering in Jeff's stomach.

Doc Parks's words were still in Jeff's head, and he was trying hard to make himself believe them, but it was difficult. Deep down, he just couldn't buy the idea that the loss of Frank Ames only made a tough job a little tougher. Bedford wasn't a one-star team. Both Paul and Jim Hall could carry the load in the guard slots,

but neither of them was even close to being of Ames's caliber. During the regular season, Frank had averaged nineteen points a game. In a way, this was like spotting Malden nineteen points even before the tap-off.

Jeff found it impossible to keep thoughts of Pinder out of his mind for any length of time. They kept coming back and coming back. Just before Parks made his talk in the dressing room, Jeff had used the pay phone in the hall outside to call the airport. There was no news. This had added to his gnawing worries and fears.

The sound of Paul's voice snapped him away from his thoughts. The warm-ups were over, and the two squads were moving off the floor. Jeff gave Paul a nervous grin and a nod and walked with the team over to the Bedford bench. A minute after that, the starting five huddled with Doc Parks in front of the bench. The coach looked for a moment at each player in turn and then spoke only one word: "Go!" They all pressed hands, and the team moved out onto the court as the roar of the crowd approached deafening proportions.

They took their positions on the floor, and a hush fell over the spectators as the referee tossed the ball up for the tap-off. Malden grabbed the ball and got a quick score on a soft jumper from fifteen feet out. The crowd roared steadily from that point on. Jeff brought the ball out and passed to Paul as he went over the center line. Paul bounced it to Joe Hern, who pivoted from his man and fed off to Jeff, going down the middle. Jeff saw the opening to Dan Logan cutting in from the corner, and threaded the needle with a hard bounce pass. Logan got it and went up high, twisting toward the basket, but the Malden man on him went up high, too, and blocked the shot. Jeff, on his way in under the basket, lunged for the loose ball, but it slid off the tips of his fingers and into Collins's hands. The big Malden guard instantly whipped the ball out to the right to a teammate, starting a three-on-two break that yielded another score for Malden. Bedford brought the ball out again, lost it, and Malden made it six points on the scoreboard.

Doc Parks called for time and met his team at the edge of the court. "You're pushing it," he told them bluntly. "Take it easy; you've got a long way to go. They're trying to kill you off quickly. Don't let them. Play it hard, but play it sure. Make them wait until you're ready, then go! All right?"

The players nodded silently and went back onto the court. When play was resumed, Doc Parks's instructions began to pay dividends. Jeff took a pass off a faked shot by Logan at the foul line and hooked the ball in from the left side to put Bedford on the scoreboard for the first time. Twenty seconds later, when an out-of-bounds pass by Malden gave the ball to Bedford, it looked like another sure two points. Paul Young took a pass from Jeff five feet in from the right corner, without a Malden player near him. But Paul failed to hit. The ball caught the rim of the basket and bounced high into the air.

193

Logan and the Malden center both climbed the board, but it was the Malden player who came down with the ball. On the way down he made a quick outlet pass to start the fast break, but Hal Allen came out of nowhere to bat the ball down and over the baseline. Jeff moved into position to pick up Collins when Malden brought the ball back in. He couldn't help but think that Frank Ames would have sunk the shot Paul had missed and added another two points to Bedford's first two.

When Malden brought the ball out, they lost no time in making up for the fast break that had been choked off. A series of crisp passes resulted in another lay-up. It seemed as if Bedford had hardly brought the ball in bounds before Malden stole it and hit with a jumper from well out on the floor. Trailing ten to two, with but a half minute left in the quarter, Bedford brought the ball out again. This time they held on to it, and Jeff, cutting past Collins on a behind-the-back dribble, drove hard for the basket and leaped high. When he saw Collins's big hand come up after the ball, he faked the shot and shoved the ball past Collins to Joe Hern, cutting in from the other side. Hern took it and sank the shot. It was a neat under-the-basket feed. The Bedford fans loved it.

As the quarter ended, they huddled with Doc Parks. "That's the way to work it!" He grinned broadly. "A couple more like that, and you're off to the races. I know you can do it. Now prove it!"

The words of praise lifted their spirits somewhat,

especially Jeff's. Mentally, he felt a lot better than he had at the start of the game. Physically, it was something else. No sooner had the fast tempo of the quarter stopped than fatigue set in. Jeff felt suddenly tired, every bit as tired as he usually felt at the end of a game. In the heat of the fast-paced action, he'd not been aware of the lumps he'd taken tangling with the solid Collins at close quarters. But he was very much aware of it now. He considered easing off and not playing Collins so tight, to conserve his energy for later.

But he did no such thing. The moment play was under way again, he threw himself into the game harder than ever. To the delight of the Bedford fans, he stole the ball right out from under Collins's nose and went all the way for his second score. And right after that, Hal Allen bombed in a beauty from the corner to close the point gap to two. Then Dan Logan grabbed a rebound off the board and started a fast break that caught Malden flat-footed and tied the score at ten-all.

Malden called for time to talk it over and let Bedford cool off. When play resumed, Malden went to work quickly and scored. Passing expertly, they got the ball down to the key, where Collins took a feed from the pivot man and cut for the basket. He went up for the shot, and Jeff went up with him in a desperate effort to block it. Unfortunately Jeff overplayed his man. He bumped Collins as the Malden star was shooting, and got the whistle. Collins's shot was good and so was the foul try awarded him.

Upset with himself, Jeff brought the ball out, determined to get two of the points back. When he had maneuvered into position for a clean shot at the basket, a bad pass from Hal Allen went by him and out-of-bounds, and Malden once more took possession of the ball. Ten seconds later they had added two more points to their score. Before the minute was up, Collins slipped by Jeff and popped the ball in for two more.

At that point Doc Parks gave Jeff, Paul, and Dan Logan a breather and sent in Hall, Dixon, and Phil Downs. Malden also made some substitutions, but Collins remained in the game. Sitting on the bench and mopping the sweat from his face, Jeff couldn't help but marvel at the star guard's strength and stamina. Collins had played every minute of the game so far, but he looked every bit as fresh and relaxed as he had at the start.

"What a player!" Jeff muttered aloud.

"Who?" asked Paul, sitting next to him.

"Collins," Jeff told him.

"Yeah," Paul grunted. "But you're not doing so badly yourself."

Jeff grimaced and flicked a finger at the scoreboard. "It doesn't say so up there."

What they watched from the bench was not pleasing. Bedford scored baskets, but for every two, Malden netted three. With the score Malden 34 and Bedford 27 and a little over two minutes left in the half, Parks sent Jeff, Paul, and Logan back in. The breather had done Jeff good, had put the spring and bounce back into him and given him a second wind. It seemed to have done the same for Paul and Dan. In the span of a little over a minute, they each hit for a score, while Malden collected only one basket. In the last seconds of the half, Jeff outsped Collins to tally with a lay-up, but Malden roared back to score two quick baskets and add a free throw. When the half-time buzzer sounded, it was still Malden in front, 41–35.

Doc Parks didn't say anything at first, when the Bedford players reached the dressing room, grim-faced. He gave them a few minutes to towel off, relax, and re-charge their batteries. When he did talk to them, it was not in generalities. He spoke to each individual player in turn. He told each what he had done right, then what he had done wrong and how best to correct the fault. There was no tongue-lashing, fist pounding, no display of any sort. He spoke quietly but straight to the point. He ended his talk with these words:

"You're six points behind at the half, but that doesn't worry me a bit. It doesn't because you've already shown me what I knew you would: that you've got what it takes to beat them, even without Frank on the floor. Win or lose, you're my kind of team. Now, let's go out and win us a state championship!"

"Right! Let's go!" Dan Logan shouted.

The others instantly echoed his words, and minutes later, when they trooped through the dressing-room doorway, there were no grim looks on their faces.

There was, instead, a fierce eagerness to get on with it and finish the job.

The second half started with Malden again grabbing the tap-off, but they did not have the ball for long— just long enough to get it upcourt for one shot. It was a jumper by Collins, but Jeff went up with him to block his shot and knock the ball down. Paul grabbed it on the first bounce and outraced his man to lay it up and in for two points.

The sudden reversal appeared to upset Malden momentarily. They brought the ball downcourt, only to lose it again when a wild pass sailed out-of-bounds. Bedford was quick to take advantage of the opportunity. Paul threw in to Jeff, who whipped it to Dan Logan in the key. He feinted a shot and fed back to Hal Allen at the edge of the circle, and he made the scoring shot. The Malden coach called for time and huddled with his team at the edge of the court. What he told them apparently settled them down, because they came out of the huddle to score quickly and collect another point on Dan Logan's third foul.

Bedford got two of the three points back when Paul scooped up a loose ball and streaked for the basket. Jeff went with him, and Collins, the lone defender, didn't stand a chance in the two-on-one situation, Paul taking a fast return pass from Jeff and going up high to drop the ball through the hoop. It was a nice bit of high-speed basketball, and the crowd yelled its approval. That roar was nothing compared to the roar that went up when Joe Hern sank a high, arching shot from the corner to close the gap to one point. Doc Parks, watching from the bench, knew that his words had ignited the vital spark. After an up-and-down first half, the team had found the groove and was playing as it had played all season long. A fast, mobile group, completely confident in their ability to pull the game out of the fire and grab themselves a win. If the Bedford coach needed further proof of his team's intentions, he got it a few moments later when Jeff hooked in a left-hander to put his team out in front by a point.

The Bedford fans in the seats went wild. The arena became a bedlam of burgeoning sound. But Malden was by no means a defeated team, or even close to it. Jeff had no sooner scored the basket that put Bedford in the lead than Malden put on a furious rally that netted them a quick four points, and they had the lead again.

Bedford fought right back. Joe Hern hit on a jumper from the outside. Then, when Bedford later regained possession, Paul, dribbling hard and fast upcourt, fired the ball to Jeff, who whipped it to Logan in the key. The tall center pushed the ball out to Allen. He cut by a screen, faked a shot when his guard slid by the pick, and passed to Paul coming in from the left for an easy score.

Before Malden could bring the ball out, the quarter ended, but seconds after the final quarter started they scored and took the lead again. Bedford promptly got

199

it back when Dolan tipped in a rebound, and then lost the lead when Collins slipped away from Jeff for a short jumper.

That was the way it went, minute after minute. First one team would score, and then the other team would score. The one-point lead bounced back and forth with almost predictable regularity. Doc Parks kept Jeff and Paul in the game but gave his front line a quick breather, one player at a time.

When there were only two minutes left in the final quarter, Bedford was in front by one slim point. Malden hit twice in quick succession to take a three-point lead. Bedford fought back furiously, and a beautiful turn-around jumper from the pocket by Joe Hern cut Malden's lead to one again.

With less than twenty seconds left, Malden brought the ball out slowly and tried to stall out the clock. Collins had the ball, eating up precious seconds on the dribble. With time running out, Collins feinted a dribble to the left, and Jeff outguessed him. He moved in close on Collins's right and shot out his hand to bat the ball away.

Collins recovered quickly as Jeff scooped up the ball. Jeff's mind raced as he noted that the Malden guard was the only defender between him and the basket. Should he chance a shot from out on the court or stake everything on beating Collins to the basket for the better percentage lay-up attempt?

Past midcourt, Jeff angled slightly to his left and

slowed his dribble, trying to suck the wily defender closer, to defend against a desperation shot from out on the court. If Collins took the bait, a sudden spurt of speed might be all Jeff needed to gain an extra step and drive all the way to the basket. Collins didn't bite but continued to backpedal toward his team's goal. He knew the percentages against a long shot as well as Jeff.

Approaching the key, Jeff renewed his speed as he decided what he would do. It had to work. . . .

Collins came up to guard against a possible jumper from the key. As he did so, Jeff tapped the ball deftly behind his back to his left hand. As Jeff had suspected, Collins was ready for it. He quickly overshifted to that side to bat the ball away. His defense was letter-perfect, except for one thing: The ball wasn't there. No sooner had the behind-the-back dribble reached Jeff's left hand than, still behind Jeff's back, it was tapped back to the right, leaving the startled Collins grabbing for nothing but air. Jeff's right-handed lay-in attempt thudded off the backboard, hung tantalizingly on the front of the rim for a long moment, and dropped through as the horn sounded—and pandemonium broke loose in the Bedford Arena.

18 Surprises

JEFF PUSHED HIS WAY toward the ramp leading down to the dressing rooms. With the game over and the state championship won, thoughts of Ben Pinder broke free and flooded his mind. All he wanted now was to get home as quickly as possible and find out if his aunt had heard any news of the missing airliner.

Some fans tried to hoist Jeff onto their shoulders, but he struggled free. Doc Parks was being carried around the court above a surge of jubilant students who were shouting and singing the school victory song. It was ten minutes before Jeff could escape the crowd.

Once inside the dressing room, he showered quickly, threw on his street clothes, jammed his basketball gear into his gym bag, and raced out the back door. As he pushed through it, Paul Young and a couple of the others yelled after him something about a victory party, but he paid no attention and hurried out of the arena toward his parked car. The traffic jam in the parking lot held him up for another fifteen minutes. He finally reached home nearly an hour after the game had ended and rushed in through the front door.

The first thing he saw was his aunt sitting in a chair by the phone with her head bent and her face buried in her hands. For one awful moment his heart felt as if it had stopped. Then he rushed across the room and dropped to his knees in front of her.

"Aunt Kate!" he cried in anguish. "What is it? Ben? Is he—"

The rest went unspoken as his aunt raised her tear-stained face. She was smiling!

"Ben is all right, Jeff," she said in a shaking voice. "I've just talked to him on the phone. He's fine!"

For a few seconds Jeff couldn't speak. Then the words came out in a rush of sound. "Ben's all right? Then why are you crying? Where is he? What happened? What'd he say?"

"He's at Winston Air Force Base in Missouri," Kate Martin told him. "That's where his plane landed. They ran into the storm, and when they lost radio contact, the pilot decided to fly around the storm area. He changed course and headed for the nearest emergency landing location, which was the Air Force base."

"That must have been plenty rough!" Jeff breathed.

"That was only part of it," his aunt said. "No sooner had they landed at Winston than the storm hit the base. Lightning knocked out the power plant, the phones, the base radio—everything. The base was completely out of contact with the rest of the world for over four hours. Once communications were restored, the passengers were allowed to use the outside phones for personal calls. That's when Ben called me."

"When's he getting here?" Jeff asked. "Did he say, or doesn't he know?"

"He said that the radio had been repaired," his aunt replied, "and they expected to take off for St. Louis in another hour or so. His guess was that he'd get to Bedford tomorrow morning. But he's not sure of the time, so we're not to meet him at the airport. As soon as he lands he'll take a taxi here."

"What about Denver?" Jeff asked. "What did he say about that?"

"Everything was fine," Kate said. "He just had some papers to sign. He'll give us the whole story when he gets here in the morning. He couldn't talk very long because there were other passengers waiting to use the phone to contact their relatives."

Jeff sat down beside his aunt and sighed. "Well, Ben

205

is all right. That's the important thing."

He noticed a strange look in his aunt's eyes when she said, "You're right, Jeff."

"Did you tell him we won the game?" Jeff asked.

"Yes," Kate replied. "I listened on the radio. He was very proud of you when I told him about it—so am I! Congratulations!"

"Thanks!" Jeff said with a grin. "It feels pretty good, believe me. Now that I know for sure that Ben is safe, it feels great!"

"Why didn't Frank Ames play?" his aunt asked. "I didn't hear what the announcer said."

Jeff told her about Ames's accident and about some of the highlights of the game. When he had finished, he realized for the first time how tired he really was. The relief of knowing that Ben was safe had relaxed him completely, and now he felt as though his bones were made of rubber.

He was asleep almost instantly when he fell into bed that night, and he slept soundly, undisturbed by the faraway noises of singing, shouting, and horn-honking still coming from the arena.

Jeff and his aunt rushed to the door when Ben Pinder arrived at nine the next morning.

"Are we glad to see you!" Jeff exclaimed.

"Indeed we are!" his aunt added.

Ben Pinder smiled at them. "The feeling's mutual, believe me!" he declared.

"Come in, Ben," Kate Martin said hurriedly. "You must be exhausted after last night. Have you had breakfast yet?"

"I had breakfast on the plane," Ben told her, stepping inside and setting down the suitcase he carried. "Thanks, just the same."

"Hey, Ben, what about Denver?" Jeff blurted out, no longer able to hold it back. "What is—"

"Jeff, for heaven's sake!" his aunt admonished. "At least give Ben a chance to catch his breath!"

Pinder laughed. "That's all right, Kate," he said to her. "I guess I'm as anxious to tell it as Jeff is to hear it."

"Well, if that's the case," she said, smiling at him, "let's all go and sit down right now."

Leading the way into the living room, she sat down on the sofa. Pinder sat down beside her, and Jeff took a chair facing them.

"Congratulations on last night's game," Ben said to Jeff. "I understand you were the star. I sure wish I could have been there."

"Thanks," Jeff replied. "I wish you could have, too. You know, now that the season's over, you may never see me play basketball again."

"I don't know about that," Ben said with a smile. "The purpose of my trip to Denver was to meet with the president and the board of regents of Clarke College, located just outside the city. Now, as you know, I took my YMCA job as a stopgap until I found what I thought was absolutely the right job for me. Well, a

207

month or so ago Clarke College offered me that job—
as athletic director of the college."

"Oh, Ben, that's wonderful!" Jeff's aunt exclaimed.

"I think so, too," Ben said, smiling at her. "I visited
the place last year when I was at the Denver Y. Clarke
is not a big college, but it has a fine academic reputation
and is growing fast. Up until now, sports have been
pretty secondary. But now they want to expand their
athletic program—particularly basketball. So that'll be
my job. Start from scratch and come up with a winning
basketball squad. I think I can. I signed the contract
Saturday morning."

"That's wonderful!" Kate Martin said again.

"Yeah," Jeff murmured, stunned. Now the full impact
of the situation had hit him. *College.* Paul would be
going to college—his family could afford it. Frank
Ames was going to college, too, on a basketball scholarship. And now Ben was leaving Bedford to take a job at
a college. Jeff felt suddenly alone. There was a moment
of embarrassing silence.

Pinder finally broke it. "Hey, Jeff, I did say that there
was something in this for you, too, remember—at the
restaurant Friday night?"

Jeff looked up, curious.

Ben took some folded papers out of the inside pocket
of his sports coat.

"How would you like to play four years of basketball
for me—and get a college education, too?"

Jeff stood up, almost knocking his chair over. "How

would I like to *what?*" he asked incredulously.

"You heard right the first time. How would you like to play basketball for me at Clarke?" Pinder repeated. "They're really serious about making a name for themselves in basketball. I have the authority to offer full-ride scholarships to promising high-school basketball players, provided they're also good students. Here." He handed Jeff a pamphlet with pictures of the Clarke campus and several information sheets explaining the new scholarship offer. "You could be the first student admitted under this new scholarship program, Jeff, if you're interested."

"Interested? *Wow!* You really mean it, Ben?"

"I sure do. Why don't you look over the pamphlet and read about it? I've got some other material for you, too, in the suitcase. You can look at it later."

"Oh, Ben, that's wonderful!" Aunt Kate took his hand.

Jeff looked up from the pamphlet excitedly and was about to speak. Ben and Aunt Kate were looking at each other, silent and smiling.

"Gee," Jeff said with a grin, "this is fantastic!"

Ben and Aunt Kate still looked into each other's eyes.

"Hey, I'm going over to Paul's and tell him the great news!"

His aunt spoke without looking away from Ben. "All right, Jeff. We'll see you later."

On the porch, Jeff stopped for a moment, lost in

thought. Ben Pinder—maybe a permanent member of the family? Not a bad idea—not bad at all!

He laughed as he headed in the direction of Paul's house.

Whitman CLASSICS

The Hound of the
  Baskervilles

Tales to Tremble By

More Tales to Tremble By

Seven Great Detective
  Stories

Black Beauty

Tales From Arabian Nights

Little Women

The Call of the Wild

Tom Sawyer

Robin Hood

The Wonderful Wizard
  of Oz

Robinson Crusoe

Wild Animals I Have
  Known

The War of the Worlds

Stand By for Adventure

Huckleberry Finn

Alice in Wonderland

REG. U.S. PAT. OFF.

*Start your home library of
WHITMAN CLASSICS now.*

Whitman ADVENTURE and MYSTERY Books

SPORTS STORIES
Throw the Long Bomb
Hot Rod Road

BRAINS BENTON
The Missing Message
The Counterfeit Coin
The Stolen Dummy
The Roving Rolls
The Waltzing Mouse
The Painted Dragon

DONNA PARKER
At Cherrydale
Special Agent
On Her Own

WALT DISNEY PRESENTS
Peter Pan
The Gnome-Mobile
The Swiss Family
Robinson

TELEVISION FAVORITES
The Mod Squad

Land of the Giants

Ironside

Mission: Impossible

Star Trek

Hawaii Five-O

The High Chaparral

The Rat Patrol

Garrison's Gorillas

The Monkees

Bonanza

Lassie·
Bristlecone Pine
Smelters' Cave

The Invaders

Gunsmoke

Whitman
REG. U.S. PAT. OFF.